DRAGON THREADS

DRAGON THREADS

A Virginia Davies Quilt Mystery
Book Nine

By
David Ciambrone

Names, characters, businesses, places, events, and incidents are either the products of the author's imagination or used in a fictitious manner. Any resemblance to actual persons, living or dead, or actual events, is purely coincidental.

No part of this publication may be reproduced, stored in a retrieval system, or transmitted in any form or by any means, electronic, mechanical, photocopying, recording, or otherwise, without the written permission of the publisher.

Text Copyright © 2023 David Ciambrone

All rights reserved.
Published 2023 by Progressive Rising Phoenix Press, LLC
www.progressiverisingphoenix.com

ISBN: 978-1-958640-35-7

Printed in the U.S.A.

Book and Cover design by William Speir
Visit: http://www.williamspeir.com

ACKNOWLEDGMENTS

Writing is a solitary affair, but any author will also tell you their writing depends on a host of others who have provided needed information, ideas, inspiration, critiques, just plain support when we needed it, and someone to listen when things go awry. To this end, I'd like to thank the following people and groups for their support bringing this book to life.

My great publisher, Amanda M. Thrasher, and the editors at Progressive Rising Phoenix Press, LLC. Without them, this book would not have seen the light of day.

The San Gabriel Writer's League mystery critique group.

My friend Cynthia Clements for the quilt that was used on the cover for the story.

My wife Kathy for her inspiration.

IN MEMORIUM

During the writing of this novel, my wonderful, loving wife, Kathy, who was an inspiration for everything I've done, passed away from cancer.

I miss her and dedicate this book and all the Virginia Davies Quilt Mysteries to her.

CHAPTER 1

Georgetown, Texas

Virginia Davies Clark sat at her desk in her cluttered museum office, with a pencil sticking out of her shoulder-length blonde hair. Her suit jacket hung on a clothes hanger on the back of her office door. She rested her forehead in her hands as she concentrated on a document on her desk. At the sound of a knock on the doorframe of her office, she jerked her head up and saw the San Gabriel Museum director. "Dr. Doverspike. You gave me a start. What can I do for you?" She glanced at her office clock. *Eight o'clock. Must be dark outside. What is Dr. Doverspike doing here at this hour? He hates driving in the dark.*

Fred Doverspike entered and plopped on a chair in front of Virginia's desk. "I have some news about Dr. Sorenson."

Virginia frowned. *Terry's supposed to be sorting through the estate of Sir Johnathan Buckman, the wealthy recluse who lived on Buckman Island—a privately owned Texas barrier island in the Gulf of Mexico. Must be nice.* "What about her? As I recall, she's identifying and categorizing ancient North and Central American native artifacts that Mr. Buckman's estate willed to the Smithsonian and us."

"You are correct my dear, but there has been a slight snag," said Doverspike.

"Snag? I don't like the sound of that."

"I just got a call from the hospital on Galveston Island. Dr. Sorenson was airlifted there by the Coast Guard last night."

Virginia stiffened. Her heart pounded in her chest. "That's a snag? Airlifted? What happened? Is she going to be okay? What can we do?"

Dr. Doverspike leaned forward. "According to the doctor I talked to, she's recovering from an ordeal at sea. The Coast Guard informed him that she was out on a thirty-foot cabin cruiser last night by herself when there was some sort of a problem. They told him the boat had severe burn marks on the outside of the hull. Terry was slightly dehydrated, had minor burns,

Dragon Threads

and a mild concussion. She was in quite a state when the Coast Guard chopper got her to the Galveston Hospital ER. She was incoherent, and her blood pressure was sky high when she arrived. She screamed, 'the light… the light… the dragon did it', then lost consciousness. She's being treated and is now asleep at the hospital."

"Will she be all right? The light?" Virginia frowned. "What do you mean the dragon did it? That's what she said? The dragon did it?"

"The doctor thinks she will be fine in a couple of days. As to the light and the dragon part, I don't know." Doverspike fidgeted in his chair. "But there is another wrinkle."

"What did she do, steal the boat?"

Doverspike laughed. "No, she didn't steal the boat."

"Then what's the added wrinkle?"

"Since she was working on this project for us and the Smithsonian, I contacted your other employer, Senior Special Agent Tom Mason, of the Smithsonian Central Security Service, about the situation. He has just activated you from a reserve special agent to active duty. You are to get down there and join Dr. Sorenson and sort this problem out."

"Right now? I want to help Terry and all, but I'm just getting this Anasazi project started." She waved her hand over the documents on her desk. "There is a lot of work to do, permits, land surveys… He has other agents in Texas he can send, and I'm preparing a grant request and—"

"Virginia, it can wait. Senior Special Agent Tom Mason has just sent our museum a sizeable… no… make that a huge grant. He's covering all your expenses, and specifically providing total funding for your project."

Virginia's eyes widened. "He did what?"

"Provided total funding for your project, my dear, and he obtained the necessary Arizona, BLM, and Park Service permits."

"That's… that's great!"

"Yes, it is. They're also paying us handsomely, yet again, for your services and your project. The museum makes a lot of money from them when you go on adventures for the SCSS, and I get to add your colorful exploits to my "The Adventures of Virginia" notebook. So now you don't need that grant request. You have the money in your account as of fifteen minutes ago."

"Tom is bribing you."

"No, generously compensating us for you to do the splendid things you accomplish for them. So, my dear, you're now back on active duty as a special agent of the SCSS. Go pack. Agent Mason needs you with Terry as quickly as possible."

Virginia pulled the pencil from her hair. "Okay. I'll lock this stuff up and get going. My husband isn't going to be happy. That *Perilous Threads* case six months ago worried him."

"I think Dr. Clark's disappointment will be somewhat alleviated," Doverspike said. "The SCCS gave him, and another professor friend of his at the University of Texas, a large grant to cover their new joint research project for the next three years. Something to do with ions and electrolytic foam. Not sure what that means."

Virginia kneaded her forehead. "They bribed Andy, too?"

"Yes, well, the Smithsonian doesn't think of it as a bribe. They see it as assisting two university professors to advance science… and smooth over any resistance to you being activated as a special agent. Now go help Dr. Sorenson. I'm sure once she's recovered, she can explain things. It shouldn't take long, and with the *two* of you on Buckman Island, what could go wrong?"

Virginia sighed. "What could go wrong? How about some mysterious lights and a fire breathing dragon?"

He gave a dismissive gesture. "I'm sure you can handle it." Doverspike slowly rose. "Damn arthritis. Getting older isn't for sissies." As he meandered out of her office, Doverspike glanced over his shoulder and said, "See if you can bring Terry's dragon here for an exhibit. Oh, did I mention the unusual quilt?"

Virginia jerked up in her chair. "No. What quilt? Unusual? What's unusual about it?"

"Terry will explain. Keep me posted. Have a nice evening."

What has Terry gotten herself into? An unusual quilt? Weird lights? A dragon? Do I need a sword to kill a dragon? Virginia sat dumbfounded. *Dr. Doverspike wants the dragon. Of course he does.* Virginia opened her desk drawer and pulled out her SCSS credentials and badge. *I'd better take more than one gun. I may also need to borrow a sword before I go.*

CHAPTER 2

The next day was sunny and warm as Virginia made the four-hour drive down to Galveston Island from Georgetown, Texas. Arriving at eleven, Virginia found the visitor's parking at the hospital and parked under a short palm tree. With a purse slung low over her shoulder, she straightened her red blouse and hoped her black slacks weren't too wrinkled from the drive as she strolled into the bright, airy lobby. She approached the woman in a blue blazer sitting behind a counter. "I would like the room number for Dr. Terry Sorenson, please."

The woman checked her computer screen. "I don't see a Dr. Sorenson on rounds now."

"Dr. Terry Sorenson is a patient. She was brought in last night by the Coast Guard."

The woman checked again and gave Virginia a condescending look. "Oh, yes, here she is. *Ms.* Sorenson is in room 202." She pointed. "The elevators are just down that hall on the right."

Virginia stomped across the lobby, down the brightly colored hall to the twin elevators. *She didn't have to be snooty.* Virginia pushed the up arrow and waited. The elevator arrived and ferried Virginia up one floor. She marched down the hallway on her left, past the nurse's station, to room 202. The door was half-closed, and she heard Terry talking inside.

"I don't care, I want to go back to work," exclaimed Terry.

"One more day," said a man's voice. "Just to insure there are no lingering effects of your concussion. One more day. I'll stop by tonight after surgery and again first thing in the morning. We'll do one more CT scan and a blood test, and if everything looks okay, I'll have you out of here before they can charge you for another day."

Virginia peeked around the door.

Terry knitted her brow. "Promise?"

"Yes. But you will have to promise me you will take it easy for a few more days after we discharge you. Rest and report back here if there are any changes to your condition."

"Okay. But I need to—"

Virginia pushed the door open and strutted into the room. The doctor and Terry turned.

Virginia shook her head and smiled. "You need to do as the doctor orders, Terry. Hello, doctor, I'm Virginia Davies Clark, Terry's friend."

"She's also my boss," grumbled Terry.

"You need to do as the doctor orders. I'll come before the chickens are up. You will need to be ready for me to remove you from here. But if, and only if, this nice doctor says you can leave. What time should I be here, Doctor?"

He turned and looked at Virginia. "Ahh... about nine... nine-thirty."

"I'll be here. And for your sake, I hope you discharge her then or she'll make you a patient as well."

He glanced at Terry. "I believe you." The doctor rose. "I'm Dr. Sullivan."

She shook the doctor's hand. "I was notified when the Coast Guard brought her in last night. I came as soon as I could. Dr. Sorenson is part of our team."

"I see. Is there anything I can do for you, Mrs. Clark?"

Virginia pulled up a chair and sat and motioned for the doctor to resume his seat. "What was her condition, and what did she say exactly last night when she arrived?"

He glanced at Terry, who had raised the back of her bed and folded her arms across her chest. Terry nodded. "Go ahead Doctor, tell her. She'll find out soon enough anyway."

"Dr. Sorenson was shaking, dehydrated, and presented with minor burns, a few small cuts and bruises, and a concussion. She was incoherent and kept yelling something about lights and a dragon. We thought that might be the result of her concussion. That can cause temporary hallucinations. She then lost consciousness in the ER. We found no broken bones and no sign of internal injuries. Her blood work didn't indicate any drugs."

Virginia looked at Terry. "She seems to be okay now, except for the bandages."

"Yes. But I want to keep her another day to be safe. Concussions can be tricky."

Virginia eyed Terry. "You will do as the doctor orders, got it?"

Terry frowned. "Yeah. The food's pretty good here. But they won't let me have any wine."

"Wine? Are you nuts? No wine for as long as the doctor says."

"Party poopers."

Virginia stood. "Thank you for the information and taking good care of Terry, Doctor."

He nodded. "See you tonight about seven, Dr. Sorenson." He walked out of the room.

Virginia pulled her chair closer to the bed. "Okay, what's with the lights and a dragon? Seriously? A dragon? Now our beloved museum director wants us to bring it there for an exhibit."

"Of course he wants the dragon. After last night, I want its head mounted on the wall in my office." Terry settled back; her auburn hair contrasted with the stark white pillow. "There have been some irregularities at Buckman Island. I was starting to investigate when... when I was attacked."

"Irregularities?"

Terry nodded.

"Okay, we'll get to the irregularities in a moment. What were you doing alone on a cabin cruiser out in the Gulf of Mexico at night? And where did you get the boat? Did you call for the Coast Guard or did someone else?"

"I took the boat from the boat shed at Buckman Manor. I'm allowed to do that. I was out about a mile and a half from shore. The sea was calm. Before I blacked out on the boat, I grabbed the radio and called a mayday on the emergency channel. The Coast Guard must have found the boat from the radio signal. I vaguely remember—my mind was in a fog—a Coast Guard guy say I was clenching the microphone so hard the talk button was still depressed, and the radio was transmitting."

"Why were you out on the water?"

"Like I said, I was following up on some... well some strange occurrences and some discrepancies at Buckman Manor. And then there were the bright, flashing lights from a way down the island... like from a lighthouse. But there is no lighthouse there. Then I was attacked by a... you're going to have me committed when I say this, but I was suddenly attacked by a fire breathing dragon. It came out of... out of nowhere. That's when all hell broke loose, and I faded into oblivion."

CHAPTER 3

Virginia sat stunned. "A fire breathing dragon? Really?"

Terry tensed. The heart monitor beeped faster. "Yes, a fire breathing dragon. Straight out of mythology... or Hollywood."

"How big was it?"

"I don't know. Big. Bigger than the boat I was in."

Virginia pulled her chair closer to the bed. "Where did it come from?"

"The Gulf of Mexico." Terry leaned against her pillow. "Right out of the water. It was terrifying. When it attacked, I passed out."

"Let me get this straight. You noticed bright lights, like from a lighthouse, coming from part of the island where there is no lighthouse and went to investigate."

Terry nodded. "Yes."

"Why didn't you go there by land?"

"There are a few swampy areas, and the terrain is rough. It's like an... an estuary of sorts, and it was dark. Not a place to be alone at night. You only see the lights at night and not every night. I saw them and tried to investigate."

"Why not go during the day?"

"I looked there when it was daylight and found nothing."

"Okay. So, because of that, you went out alone, at night, on a cabin cruiser to investigate... and a fire breathing dragon attacked you."

Terry bolted up. "Yes. That's it exactly!"

"Anything else? Dr. Doverspike mentioned something about irregularities with the collection you were cataloging."

"Yeah, like I said, I found a *real,* disarticulated skeleton wrapped in a quilt in the attic, some of the more peculiar items in the inventory are missing, and there are some artifacts that don't look like what you'd expect from an explorer. They look more like... treasure. I'd say they are from Great Britain, only really old."

Virginia raised an eyebrow. "How old is really old?"

Terry sighed. "If you force me to guess, I'd say mid to late 1100s."

Dragon Threads

"Oh boy. This just got a whole lot stranger." Virginia placed her hand on Terry's arm. "Why didn't you call for help earlier? A skeleton could mean a murder. That's more than anyone should be responsible for alone."

Terry closed her eyes. "I know. But I didn't have anything concrete to go on. Well, besides the missing items, the out of place... things, and the skeleton wrapped in the quilt."

"Did you call the police about the skeleton?"

"No. I notified the Smithsonian. I wanted time to examine it, and figured the local sheriff would frown on that."

"You're right about that."

A nurse came rushing into the room, took Terry's blood pressure, and looked at the heart monitor. She then turned to Terry. "Your BP is too high, and your pulse rate set off the alarms at the nurse's station. You need to get some rest. No more excitement for now." She looked at Virginia. "I think your visiting time is over. She needs rest."

Virginia rose. "I think my questions about last night upset her. I'll be going, but I'll return in the morning as planned." She patted Terry's hand. "Take a nap and relax, you're not alone on this case anymore."

Terry nodded. "Okay. Just knowing you're here will be a big stress reliever. See you in the morning. Oh, one more thing. The quilt has a dragon on it and there is an inscription in Latin."

"It does?" Virginia frowned. "What does it say?"

"Virdes dracones de caelo."

"English, please."

"There be green dragons from the sky," Terry said.

Virginia left the hospital and drove to the mainland, heading north for several miles to the steel bridge that transversed over a quarter-mile expanse of water from the mainland to Buckman Island. At the island end of the bridge was an orange and white striped barrier gate and a guard station. She stopped and rolled down her window as the armed, uniformed guard stepped out of the concrete guard building. "Hi, I'm Virginia Davies Clark. I believe I'm expected."

The guard checked his tablet computer. "Yes, ma'am. This says you're with the Smithsonian. Do you have some ID?"

Virginia displayed her SCSS gold badge and credentials.

"Special agent?"

"Yes, I'm here to work with Dr. Sorenson."

He leaned on the car. "I heard she was injured last night. Do you know if she will be okay?"

"Yes. I'm going to try and bring her back from the hospital in the morning."

He straightened. "That's good. We've had some visitors and archeologists in the past who have been a real pain in the rear, but Dr. Sorenson is nice. She's friendly, answers questions, and is always respectful. She told me the island was first inhabited by Paleo-Indians. I never knew that, and I grew up around here."

"That's her. I'll get her back here as quick as I can. Then she and I have some work to do."

"I hope you can help her," the guard said. "There have been some strange things going on in the past six months."

Virginia looked at the guard's name badge. "I'll want to talk to you more about that… Frank Long. Will you be around?"

He nodded. "Yes. I live on the mainland but I'm here every weekday from nine to six. Usually out here, but some days I'm at the main compound or patrolling."

"Good. I'll find you. Now, can you tell me where to go?"

"Yes." he pointed. "Go straight for a mile to the Y. Take the right fork another two miles to the main compound. The manor house is there on a forty-foot rise along with other buildings. You're expected."

Virginia glanced out the front window. "How big is this island?"

"Buckman Island is five miles long and two and a half miles wide. It is privately owned."

"How long has the island belonged to the Buckmans, Frank?"

"For over a hundred and twenty years. Johnathan Buckman recently passed away, and he had no children. There is a cousin. I understand he'll become the new Lord of the Manor. From what I heard, he wants to do something with the place and has donated the artifact collection to a museum in Georgetown, Texas, and the Smithsonian."

Virginia smiled. "Thanks for the information. Talk to you later."

Virginia drove up the road past croton, Pan American balsam scale, flat sedge, sea purslane, beach morning glory, yellow oleanders, and scattered Royal and Washingtonia palms. When she located the Buckman manor house, she drove up the inclined driveway, studying the four-story, stone manor house with heavy metal roof. It was surrounded by palms and shrubbery. Off to the right stood a matching stone carriage house, and two stone barns sat further back. A gravel walkway wound between the buildings, toward the Gulf of Mexico and a red metal boathouse. She turned into the circular driveway, pulled up in front of the big house, and stopped. She turned toward the front of the building when the massive front door swung open. A tall, thin man emerged. He had reddish hair, parted in the middle, and he was dressed in tan slacks and a green polo shirt. Virginia chuckled. *The guard called ahead I see.*

He hurried down the brick steps to Virginia's car and stopped. "Special Agent Clark?"

"Yes."

He opened her door and helped her out. "I understand you are working with Dr. Sorenson."

Virginia nodded. "That's correct."

"I see. Let me get your bags, and if you will follow me, I'll show you to your room. When you are ready, I can give you a tour of Buckman manor and the grounds. I'm sure Dr. Sorenson will give you the island tour upon her return."

"Fine. And who are you?" She removed her suitcase from the rear of her new black Toyota Highlander.

"I am James Thornwood IV. I am the overseer and caretaker of the Buckman estate and the island."

"You're the majordomo?"

He raised an eyebrow. "I hadn't thought of it that way, but, in a word, yes."

"I see. Okay, after the tour and I get settled, I would like to ask you some questions."

"I will make myself available. Just give me a call. There is a notebook in your suite with all the important phone numbers. Dinner is served at seven p.m. and breakfast is at six a.m.. Both are in the main dining room." He picked up her bag and led her up the stone steps and into the manor house.

Virginia was awestruck as she entered the enormous, dark wood-paneled entrance hall.

"In case you are wondering," said Thornwood, "the manor has been renovated and extended over the years to create a medley of styles and designs. The house is comprised of eight bedrooms, five bathrooms, dining room, ballroom, drawing room, office, conservatory, kitchen-pantry-diner, and an entrance hall... which we are in. It also has a library, laundry room, dormer rooms in the attic, and an armory. There is a swimming pool in the rear yard."

"Interesting." Virginia glanced around at the solid maple and oak furniture that appeared to be centuries old and polished to a shine. A gilded frame hanging above a side table held an old portrait of a late 19th century dour-faced man. A huge crystal chandelier hung from above. In front of her was a wide, grand sweeping oak staircase leading upstairs that would have done well in any English manor or southern antebellum home. Various rooms were set to both sides of the entrance hall.

"As I said before, I'll give you a tour when you are ready. I'll also show you Dr. Sorenson's work area."

"That would be nice, thank you. Where are the bedrooms?"

Thornwood pointed toward the stairs. "Your suite and Dr. Sorenson's are on the top floor, near the master's suite. The other bedrooms are on the third floor."

Virginia looked up. "It's on the fourth floor?" *Maybe it's got a view of Terry's lights. But four floors? I need to hit the gym more.*

"Yes. If you follow me, we will proceed to the elevator. It was added about four years ago, and trust me, that was none too soon."

"Is the attic on the fifth level?"

"No. It's down the hall from the suites, through a steel door with two special locks. Dr. Sorenson and I have the keys."

Virginia followed him. *Steel door?* "Why a steel door?" Virginia asked.

"That's where the art and artifacts are kept, and where Dr. Sorenson is working on them," Thornwood answered.

She glanced around as they walked. "How does this place hold up in a hurricane? And shouldn't the artifacts be on a lower floor? Like during a hurricane or tornado?"

"It holds up quite well," Thornwood stated with a hint of pride. "We have been hit with some serious hurricanes in the past. But we survived. The walls are two feet thick and made of stone and steel-reinforced concrete It can withstand a category 5 hurricane and an EF 5 tornado. The roof is steel and welded to the supports, which are set in forty feet of concrete. Our doors, as you noticed, are quite thick and made of oak laminated to a steel core with multiple two-inch locking bolts. The windows are double paned, comprised of hurricane glass and three inches of Lexan. During a storm, steel shutters are deployed, covering all windows and doors. We have backup generators and satellite phones. The outbuildings are constructed in a similar fashion. Our little island has several freshwater wells, so we are not dependent on the mainland for water during a storm. The base of the building is forty feet above sea level and far enough from the ocean to not worry about wave damage or storm surge. There are a few areas of dense vegetation in the marshes to help provide additional protection from the sea. In other words, we are like a fortress."

Virginia stopped and watched Thornwood push the button for the elevator. *A fortress indeed. If you're going to live alone on a barrier island, I guess you need something like this. But it does seem like overkill. It's more like a bank vault. What are they really protecting?*

CHAPTER 4

Virginia entered her suite and looked around. *This room is larger than half my house. Love the four-poster bed. Nice bathroom. The view of the Gulf of Mexico is great.* After unpacking, she slipped out into the hallway, turned, and walked to the steel door. She put her hand on it. *This looks like a bank vault. I'll check it out after Terry returns.* Virginia took the elevator back to the first floor and stepped into the living room that looked like something from an English manor.

The walls were walnut paneled. A bookcase took up one whole wall. The coffered ceiling and stone fireplace featured symbols from the Book of Kells. A large window overlooked the well-manicured grounds, and farther across the sand, the wild scrub brush of the island. McDonnell tartan plaid carpets sat atop a polished hardwood floor. On the wall opposite the fireplace resided a built-in bookcase. Heavy leather chairs, massive end tables, and a large square coffee table were strategically placed in front of the huge stone fireplace, with a painting of the first Buckman Island owner, Sir Robert Buckman, hanging above the mantel. Chiseled into the front of the stone mantel was *Virdes dracones de caelo.* "There be dragons. On the quilt and cut into the stone?" she mumbled to herself. "I need to talk to James Thornwood." She jumped at the voice behind her.

Thornwood stood in the doorway. "May I be of assistance, madam?"

Virginia pointed at the mantle. "Dr. Sorenson told me about a quilt with a dragon on it and these words. Is there a special meaning for that phrase to be in both locations?"

"There be green dragons from the sky." He motioned at one of the leather wingchairs in front of the fireplace. "Please have a seat. Yes, there is some history. Let me tell you about it."

"Okay." Virginia sat in the chair facing the fireplace.

Thornwood sat in the one next to her with the end table between them. He sighed. "The story goes that when the Buckmans lived in England there was a dragon on their estate. Since before 1066, the family lived at the manor in harmony with the beast. Around 1750, the Buckmans started collecting relics from around the world. They were mostly holy and ancient relics, and his methods were... sometimes not... ethical or legal. In the early 1900s, the Buckman Lord of the Manor, Sir Robert Buckman, suddenly moved to Texas along with his collection of relics and antiquities. Sir Robert's brother, Lord Manfred Buckman, became the Lord of the Manor in England after Sir Robert moved here."

Virginia turned. "Why'd he move?"

"I don't know the whole story, but I heard it was to escape some legal entanglements. There may have been a lady involved."

"Okay, then what?"

"He widened the Buckman collections to include New World artifacts from North America, Central America, and South America."

Virginia stared at the fireplace. "I see. And the dragon?"

Thornwood hesitated, then said, "According to the story, it came with him."

Virginia sat, stunned. "Really? A dragon came with him? Why didn't it stay in England? Is there a Buckman dragon still in England today?"

"Yes, family lore and witnesses say there is still a dragon or dragons reported to be on the estate in England, or so I'm told. For all I know, they're related to the dragon here."

"If there is still a dragon here, then the one in 1900 had to have had a mate and offspring or they would be dead by now, wouldn't they?"

"You're right. Maybe there were a couple of them that migrated, or there could have been a Texas dragon cousin living here. No one has thought of that angle before you. And for the record, I don't know how long dragons live."

"How did a dragon migrate from England with Sir Robert? US Customs would probably notice a dragon, probably without a passport, walking down a gangway getting off a ship, or resting in a crate."

Thornwood bit his lip then slowly nodded. "One would think so. Maybe the dragon or dragons flew."

"That's a long flight. I hope they got air miles." Virginia asked, "Have you seen this alleged dragon?"

"Well, yes and no. I've heard the stories. I've seen what appeared to be a dragon just off the coast and on the island to our north. The appearances were at night so..."

"Yeah, I get it. It could be a dragon who is a night owl, but then there is the problem that dragons don't exist," said Virginia.

"Correct. But there are footprints left in wet sand, strange noises, burnt tree stumps, and sightings by people on the mainland."

"Sightings by others?"

Thornwood nodded. "Over the decades there have been sightings of what was reported to be a dragon."

"Flying?"

"Flying, on the ground, and in the water."

"Why didn't this make the news?"

"It did a long time ago." Thornwood took a breath. "There were a few investigations that didn't go anywhere, especially since the dragon didn't hurt anyone, and the Buckmans wouldn't allow any investigators on the island."

"The locals could have made the dragon a tourist attraction. Money usually wins over resistance."

"A few tried it, but they never succeeded. They couldn't get access to the island, and the ones who tried to use boats... well that approach didn't turn out well. The dragon sightings dwindled for a time, so interest diminished."

"So, the Buckman dragon could be the Texas version of the Loch Ness Monster."

"Yes, but he doesn't look like Nessie. He looks like a dragon."

Virginia sat back staring at the fireplace. "Does this Buckman family dragon have a name?"

Thornwood chuckled. "It's Harry."

"Harry?" Virginia rubbed the bridge of her nose. "You've got to be kidding."

"Nope. His name is Harry."

"Okay, Harry the Dragon. I have another question. Dr. Sorenson said there's a skeleton in the collection wrapped in a quilt. Do you—"

Thornwood stiffened. "She said there's a what?"

"A skeleton. A human skeleton."

He jumped to his feet. "I... I. No. I had no idea. Did she notify the sheriff? What should I do?"

"No, she didn't contact the sheriff. I'm a federal agent assigned to assist Dr. Sorenson in this matter by Washington. I'll talk to the sheriff later."

Thornwood nodded slightly. "I see." He resumed his seat.

"Dr. Sorenson will be back tomorrow and I'm sure between the two of us... and possibly you, we can figure this out. Your help will be appreciated." Virginia stood, stepped to the fireplace, and turned. "Let me change the subject for a minute. How did the last 'Texas' Buckman die?"

"That was Sir Johnathan Buckman. He died of old age. He was 98. He had a heart problem and COPD."

"Who owns the Texas Buckman estate now?"

"That would be Sir Edward Buckman." Thornwood closed his eyes for a moment. "He's the son of the late Sir Johnathan Buckman, and Sir Edward was on a business trip in England when his father died. Sir Edward is on his way from England as we speak."

"I'll need to speak with Sir Edward when he gets here," Virginia said.

"Of course, Agent Clark, I'll arrange it."

"That's a lot of Buckman sirs. How'd they all become knights?" asked Virginia to try and relax Thornwood.

"They aren't knights." Thornwood adjusted his tie. "They're baronets."

Virginia frowned. "What's a baronet?"

"It's like an inherited knight's title. Actually, a baronet is one rank below a baron in the ranks of heraldry."

"Interesting. You mentioned Sir Edward was on a business trip. What does he do for a living?" asked Virginia.

Thornwood gave her a blank stare. "I don't know. He is rather closed-mouth about his finances and business dealings."

"Since you knew him, what did Sir Johnathan do for a living?"

"I'm not sure. Sir Johnathan and Sir Edward were quite reluctant to share anything about their personal financial situations or their business relations."

Virginia nodded. "We have our work cut out for us."

Thornwood leaned forward. "I'll do what I can to assist in your investigations. I'm sure Sir Edward would agree."

"One more thing, how many are on staff here?"

"There's the cook, two housekeepers, two gardeners, six security guards, and me."

"I see. Thank you for all the information." Virginia turned toward the window and spotted a sailboat. *Funny, Thornwood doesn't know what business they're in. I'd better call the SCSS and get a background check on the staff, Sir Edward, and Sir Johnathan. We'll see just how cooperative Sir Edward really is when he gets here.*

CHAPTER 5

At nine-thirty the following morning Virginia strolled into Terry's hospital room and found Terry standing next to the bed adjusting her light blue t-shirt and smoothing her tan slacks.

Virginia stopped. "You're dressed already? Did the doctor discharge you yet?"

"Yes. He was here at five-thirty. They did another CT scan of my head and drew blood. The doctor said everything checked out okay. He said he doesn't think there will be any long-term problems related to my concussion, but I need rest to be on the safe side. He gave me a list of things I need to watch for, like this headache I have. Paperwork is done, and accounting is happy." She held up a plastic baggie. "Got my drugs from the hospital pharmacy that the Doc said I needed, so I'm ready to get out of here."

"Good. Let's go." As they left the room, Virginia said, "I was at Buckman Manor yesterday after I left you. I met James Thornwood IV. He is a spring of local knowledge."

"Yes, and he's extremely loyal to the Buckmans."

"I inquired about any resident dragons."

"Oh boy." Terry's expression grew guarded. "He told you the history?"

"Yep. He seems to believe it."

"After the other night I might be joining him as a believer."

Virginia helped Terry into the car and drove out of the hospital. "Let me see if I've got everything straight. You found some irregularities in the artifacts and relics collection, saw a strange light and a resident temperamental dragon, and you found a human skeleton in a quilt."

"That pretty much sums things up." Terry chuckled. "But you'll just love the quilt."

Virginia drove over the bridge off Galveston Island and turned north toward Buckman Island. "Why? Because it says 'there be dragons' on it? What else is unusual about the quilt?"

"It's got an image of a dragon on it."

Virginia rolled her eyes. "Of course it does. Now, about the skeleton. What can you tell me about it?"

Terry leaned back in her seat; her face scrunched in concentration. "Man, sometimes just thinking hurts. The skeleton is a male. Caucasian. Age between sixty and seventy when he died. He was about five-feet-ten inches tall and probably weighed over two-hundred pounds. He had the indications of a healed broken arm and a rib. The injuries were old. He also had arthritis in his right hip, his neck, both hands, back... he has osteoarthritic lipping. He had periostitis in his ulna. A few bones were stained. His jaw and teeth exhibited several dental caries... cavities and some periodontal disease. He wasn't big on visiting his dentist."

"That's pretty detailed. It sounds like he had a rough life. What did he die of?"

Terry lifted one shoulder in a semblance of a shrug. "I don't know. I've just got the skeleton, no soft tissue. He could have died of one of several illnesses or could have been killed. Whatever it was, it didn't affect the bones."

Virginia wound her way through traffic. "How long did you examine the skeleton?"

"About a half hour. That was after I laid him out on a table, so his bones were in their proper locations."

"That was fast. You said he was wrapped in the... the dragon quilt? How'd he fit? Was the quilt big?"

"No, it's closer to a lap quilt. But remember, the skeleton was disarticulated. I had to put him back together."

"Oh yeah. So, we should call the sheriff."

"Not so quick. His dental work, plus other signs, indicated to me he died a little over a hundred years ago, around 1920s to mid-thirties. He's of more interest to me than the sheriff. If he was murdered, the killer is most likely already dead. Anyway, you're a federal special agent, and you were sent here by the Smithsonian Central Security Service. So, you and I will do the necessary investigations."

Virginia glanced at Terry. "For just getting out of the hospital with a head injury, you're pretty bossy."

Terry laughed, then cringed. "Maybe I should have stayed in the hospital." She closed her eyes and sighed. "Your boss at the SCSS, Special Agent Tom Mason, called me just before you arrived. He activated my..." she made air quotes... "enhanced Special Police status with the Smithsonian Police so I can continue to do what I was sent here to do and also assist you. We are the police in this case."

"Tom called you?"

"He called to see how I was doing, and when I told him about everything, he activated me. He said we make a good team."

"He's right. We do make a great team."

"I know. Tom said he was going to call or text you but had to go to a meeting."

Virginia stopped at a traffic light. "Are you armed? Do you have your special police credentials and badge with you?"

"Yes. They are locked in a metal box in my suitcase at the manor."

"Good. You may need them. Let's stop for breakfast. How about that Cracker Barrel over there?"

"Sounds good. I'm starving. I didn't get to eat breakfast at the hospital this morning," Terry said.

"I hope the people in the car following us have had their breakfast. They could be in for quite a wait, and it's going to get hot out here."

CHAPTER 6

After breakfast, Virginia and Terry drove toward Buckman Island. Terry watched the car trailing them. "So far, they haven't tried anything. I wonder who they are and why they're following us?"

"I don't know. Maybe they think you discovered something on Buckman Island," Virginia said. "Or they could be looking for information about your dragon. Want to find out?"

"No. The hospital doctor said no excitement, and dealing with the people who are following us sounds like just that… excitement."

"Okay. We'll lose them." Virginia accelerated.

"Good." Terry looked out the window at the clouds. "Look, the sky is nearly black, even though it is only mid-morning. We're in for a blow. How about we just go to the island. We can arrange for a play date with them some other time." Terry gripped her seatbelt as Virginia fishtailed around a corner and tore down a side street. "Where are you going?"

"Toward the marina over there." Virginia sped along the narrow street, swung into a parking lot next to a large two-story building, and slid into a space between a truck and the building facing the marina. "Take a look." She pointed at the car slowly prowling the street. The car parked across the street in front of the marina. Two men in suits climbed out and looked around. One of the men spotted Virginia's Highlander and pointed. The two men jogged toward the car.

"I don't like this," Virginia said. "I guess we can either run them over or talk to them."

Terry stared at the oncoming men. "I need some more meds. My head hurts. Right now, running them over sounds good."

The men slowed and approached Virginia's vehicle. She lowered her side window while fishing her semiautomatic from her backpack and setting it on top of the console between the seats. Out of the corner of her eye, she spotted Terry removing something from the glove box.

The men stopped a few feet away. The taller of the two men stepped forward and opened a badge case holding a gold badge. "U.S. Customs.

We'd like a word."

Terry folded her arms across her chest and leaned toward the window. "What do you want?"

"We need a little information."

Virginia looked at the sky. "It's going to rain. Give us your cards and we'll contact you tomorrow."

Terry held up her hand. "Before we go, I want to know exactly what you want."

"We are investigating some antiquities smuggling and think you might be able to help us." The agent looked at the rolling black clouds. "We could go to that coffee shop across the street and talk."

Unmoved, Terry asked, "Why would we be able to help you?"

"You have access to Buckman Island and the manor."

"Give us your contact information and we'll call you."

Virginia tilted her head. "Can I see your badges and credentials again, please?"

The shorter agent frowned. "Why?"

"Because those look like older badges, and I didn't get a good look at your credentials."

"Look, lady, we're wasting time." He stepped closer to the car.

Virginia released her seatbelt and pulled her SCSS gold badge out and flashed it. "Special Agent, SCSS. Now about those badges."

The men spun around and jogged back to their car.

Virginia chuckled. "Something I said?"

Terry watched the men run. "Yeah. Special agent and your gold badge. He may have spotted your gun sitting here, or this." She held up a .38 revolver.

Virginia raised an eyebrow. "Where did you get that?"

"It's yours. It was in your glove box." Terry glanced around. "We've got more company coming."

A man with graying black hair, dressed in a blue blazer and tan slacks standing next to the building watched the two men getting into their car. He turned and approached Virginia's vehicle. He stopped next to the car. "Excuse me. I watched what happened and heard you are federal agents. Is that correct?"

Virginia nodded. "Yes, sir. I'm Special Agent Virginia Davies Clark and this is Agent Terry Sorenson of the Smithsonian Central Security Service."

"Nice to meet you, ladies." He pointed at the two fake customs men. "I hope you're investigating those two. They're not real police, they are suspected smugglers. Bad apples, them. The sheriff and Texas Rangers could never get enough on them to warrant an arrest. Now that they've impersonated federal officers, you can arrest them."

"You know them?"

"Yes. The tall thin one is Brian Kinman. The other gentleman is John McDougal. Losers both. They have an old fishing boat they use for smuggling, and they live aboard."

Terry frowned. "What were they allegedly smuggling?"

"Drugs, antiquities, and sometimes people."

"Them? They don't seem bright enough to mastermind a successful smuggling operation."

He sighed. "You're right. They're the hired help. No one knows who the leader is."

Virginia tilted her head. "May I ask who you are, sir?"

"I'm sorry, I should have introduced myself. I'm Commodore Richard Haring of the Lost Harbor Yacht Club." He pointed at the building with the name of the club in blue letters on it. Our offices are right over there. This is our parking lot. Feel free to stop by anytime and have a drink on me."

Virginia eyed the building. "Thank you, we will."

Terry kneaded her forehead. "I know this will sound silly, but have you ever heard of a dragon around here?"

Commodore Haring nodded. "You must be referring to Harry. He's the Buckman dragon."

Terry sat with a blank expression. "He's got a name?"

"Yes. Some of the locals refer to him as Harry T. Dragon. The T is for terrible."

"I was going to tell you about his name later," mumbled Virginia.

"I heard Harry attacked some woman on a boat the other night," Commodore Haring said. "I hope the lady is okay. Harry is not well liked by the local chamber of commerce and some of the fishermen. He's bad for business."

"I bet." Terry swallowed. "Have you seen… Harry?"

Commodore Haring took a quick glance at the Gulf of Mexico. "At a distance. It was at night. I think it was Harry. I never got up close, thank God. Most of those that have had close encounters usually don't live to repeat the tale."

CHAPTER 7

After arriving back at Buckman Island through a rainstorm and stowing her car in the carriage house, Virginia and Terry went to the manor's library. Rain pelted the window. A fire set in the massive fireplace gave off a warm glow. Terry wandered around the room, taking in the tall dark oak bookshelves filled with volumes of hardback books of varying vintages and topics. She glanced at Virginia, who was seated in an upholstered wingchair and sipping a cup of tea by the fireplace. Terry slowly walked to the fireplace and sat in a matching chair. "I love this room. It's… restful."

"Yes, it is a nice place to relax."

"Relax?" Terry chuckled. "Bite your tongue. It's bad enough that we have a dragon, who likes to barbeque people, and an old skeleton, so please don't find any dead bodies and make things worse. You have a habit of doing that."

"I'll try. I'd like to see your workroom, the dragon quilt, and the skeleton."

"No problem." Terry took a drink of her tea. "When is Sir Edward arriving?"

"I don't know. Thornwood said he was on his way back here from England. I'll have to ask when Sir Edward is expected." Virginia set her empty cup on the table between the two chairs. "While we are in the workroom or vault for the relics, I'd like an update on the irregularities in the collection as well."

Terry finished her tea and rose. "Okay. Let's get to it."

Terry unlocked the workroom's steel door. "Your keys to the lab are inside. Everything is in here. Well, everything but the dragon."

Virginia followed Terry inside. As they entered, the positive pressure of the climate-controlled air flowed over them. The overhead lights came on automatically, illuminating a vast storeroom of antiquities, paintings, sculptures, and relics. Virginia closed the door behind her and stopped, taking in the space. "Wow. That is some collection. She stepped to a glass cabinet and peered inside at a small stone figure. "Olmec?"

Terry nodded. "Yes. There are more Mesoamerican artifacts around here, as well as artifacts from North, Central, and South America... along with some European relics." She pointed at a chart on the wall next to the door. "That chart shows the layout of the room with locations of the collection's contents."

Virginia shook her head. "I never would have guessed this collection was so large. It rivals some museums. I could get lost for days in here. Where are the skeleton and the dragon quilt?"

Terry pointed toward the rear of the room. "I've set up my workspace and tools back there." She led Virginia around displays, cabinets, and racks to the area she had selected for her workspace. She stopped next to a stainless-steel table and waved her hand over the bones laid out on the surface. "Here he is." Terry plopped on a lab stool and closed her eyes. "Not quite myself yet, sorry."

"That's okay. Take things slow for a while." Virginia leaned over and examined the remains. "Well, we've got a reassembled skeleton. I think your analysis is about as complete a picture as we're going to get from them for now."

Terry nodded. "We should notify the sheriff. I can give him the bones, the pictures I took..." She reached for a red folder near the skeleton's head, "and my analysis of the skeleton."

Virginia bit her lip. "Before we do that, I'd like to do some research into the timeframe you said he most likely died and see if there are any missing persons reports or unresolved deaths around here then."

"We could ask the sheriff to do it when we turn over the skeleton. Being feds who want to cooperate with the local fuzz goes a long way toward making useful local law enforcement friends. We can tell the sheriff about our two fake customs guys at the marina as well," Terry said.

"You have a point. Okay, I'll call the sheriff, but in the meantime, see if you can get any viable material for a DNA test. I'd like to collect that before we turn him over to the sheriff. We'll handle the DNA testing ourselves."

"Okay. I'll get right on it. But first, over here is the dragon quilt." Terry took Virginia to another table with the lap quilt displayed on it.

Virginia examined the quilt. "It's not that old. The fabric is this century. The thread count is high, and it's quality quilting fabric. So, it wasn't made in the 1920s or thirties when they used feed sacks, old clothes, and lower grade fabrics because of the depression. The actual quilting on this was machine done. The piecing work is quite good. The binding is perfect. The design is unique. I'll need to study this more. This is a work of art."

Terry looked at the quilt. "You can tell all that from your brief examination?"

"You got a lot from just looking at bones. This is my forte."

"Gotcha. I'll go look for useable material for the DNA test. I've got a sterile glove box with dry nitrogen to gather it in. I'll use a tooth. Are you going to send it to the SCSS?"

"Yep. But I think I'll call Tom Mason at the Smithsonian, while you do that, and ask for background checks and information on Thornwood and Sir Edward Buckman. Maybe the rest of the clan as well."

Terry walked to a metal cabinet and opened it. She removed a tray with small stainless-steel tools, a bone saw, a couple collection vials, and a battery powered drill, like a Dremel tool. "I'll sterilize these then get to work on the DNA extraction." As she closed the doors she stopped. She slowly said, "Virginia… come… over… here… please."

Virginia hustled between the displays and worktables to Terry. "What's wrong?"

Terry set the tray down and pointed.

Virginia looked where Terry pointed. On the floor lay the body of a well-dressed man. Virginia carefully stepped to the body and knelt. She pressed her finger to his carotid artery, then looked at Terry. "He's dead."

CHAPTER 8

Terry sighed. "I guess this would be a good time to call the sheriff."

"First, let's get Thornwood up here and see if he can identify the corpse."

"Okay. I'll go get him," Terry said. "In the meantime, a call to Senior Special Agent Tom Mason at the SCSS would be in order."

"Agreed. While you get Thornwood, I'll see if the guy has any ID on him, then call Tom." Virginia found a box of plastic gloves and slipped them on, then carefully searched the body for a wallet. She found it in his rear pants pocket and opened it. *His British driver's license says he's Sir Edward Buckman. He was the new owner of the island. Where is his passport?* She looked at his face and body features. She sniffed around his mouth. *I've smelled this before. Coffee and Tetrahydrozoline. Poisoned by eye drops.* Virginia pulled her cell phone out of her pocket and took pictures of the body and the skeleton. Then she dialed Tom Mason's number.

"Mason," Tom said as he answered the phone.

"Tom, this is Virginia Davies Clark in Texas."

"And how are things along the coast? How's Terry doing?"

"Her concussion was worse than she thought. She's still a little confused and has some pain."

"Want me to order her back to the hospital?"

Virginia chuckled. "You know she won't go. I'll keep close tabs on her, but we have a situation."

"Who did you kill?" Tom asked with a forlorn voice.

"No one." Virginia hopped onto a worktable. "Terry did a good job with the skeleton she found. We'll send you what she discovered. But we now have a fresh dead body on the floor. Terry is getting someone to confirm the identity of the corpse before we notify the sheriff. An old skeleton is one thing, but a still warm dead body is harder to explain."

"I see. Does the dearly departed have any ID on him?"

"Yes. His British driver's license says he's Sir Edward Buckman. I'm texting you the pictures I took now. Oh, one other thing. He died of Tetrahydrozoline poisoning, eye drops."

"How do you know that? Would it take much?"

"I've seen it before. And before you ask, I haven't used it to kill anyone. As to the amount, about four small vials would do it, but you need to put it in something like coffee or a flavored drink to somewhat hide the taste. In Sir Edward's case, it was coffee."

"But you could smell it?"

"Yes. Like I said, I've seen this before."

"Okay." Tom mumbled, to himself or someone in his office, something Virginia couldn't understand, and he then told her to wait. A moment later, he returned. He cleared his throat. "Okay. Your original assignment hasn't changed, but you and Terry are now to investigate the death of Sir Edward. I got clearance from Scotland Yard and our state department for your involvement with Sir Edward's murder."

"That was fast. This will go over well with the local sheriff."

"Because Scotland Yard had some intelligence that something was off about Sir Edward's activities of late, they alerted us. It has something to do with a centuries old missing royal treasure. I just texted my counterpart at the Yard what you just told me about Sir Edward. Now you're their *and* my agent in this investigation. You and Dr. Sorenson. The sheriff can either work with you, or he'll feel the pressure from Washington and London. Your status is being sent to the sheriff as we speak."

"So, I'm a Scotland Yard Detective Inspector?" Virginia asked in a chipper voice.

"Don't push it. The day I let you ladies go to work for another organization is the day the earth will stand still," Tom said.

"You might want to send that authorization to our phones and emails, too. Just so we have it in case the sheriff gets uppity."

Tom chuckled. "Okay, Detective Inspector."

Virginia thought about the day so far. "Tom, I'll text you a list of people I'd like background checks on, especially Sir Edward."

"Send the list and Terry's report on the skeleton and I'll get right on it."

"We're getting some samples from the skeleton. I'd like to get a DNA report run on it as well."

"The skeleton's DNA? Send the sample by courier to me. I'll do what I can. Good luck."

Virginia disconnected as Terry and Thornwood entered the room. Terry led Thornwood to the body and pointed. She glanced at him. "Do you recognize this man?"

Thornwood visibly shook. His uptight demeanor crumbled. He leaned on a table for support. "That... that is Sir Edward. What's he doing here? Is he... dead?"

"Yes, he's dead." Terry took Thornwood's arm and steered him to a lab stool. "Sir Edward was coming here, wasn't he? I thought you said you were picking him up at the Houston airport."

"Yes." Thornwood swallowed. "But I got a message to fetch him at eight tomorrow morning."

Virginia raised an eyebrow. "If that's the case, what's he doing here now?"

"How did he get here without you knowing about it?" Terry asked.

Thornwood looked at the two women with reddened eyes. "I don't have the answers to your questions. I'm sorry, but I don't know."

Virginia looked around the room. "This room was locked when we got here. Did he have keys to the place?"

"Yes, but I hold them when he's gone. He didn't take them to England on his trip. I just now put them back in his rooms."

Virginia shrugged. "Well, someone let him in. I'll call the gate guard, Frank Long, and see what he knows."

Thornwood sat in shock then mumbled, "Frank may be able to tell us when and how Sir Edward got on the island, but he doesn't have his keys to this part of the manor. Like I said, I just put them in his suite."

"Does anyone else besides you and Terry have access to this area?" Virginia asked.

"No. Well… you do now."

Virginia thought for a moment then said, "Mr. Thornwood, please call Frank Long and have him come here post haste. Get someone else to cover for him at the gate."

Thornwood nodded. "As you wish."

"I'll call the sheriff. Terry, you question Frank Long in the library, then question the rest of the staff. When the sheriff's people arrive, we'll introduce them to your skeleton and Sir Edward."

Terry shook her head. "That's going to be fun."

CHAPTER 9

Virginia sent the list of names for the background checks to Tom Mason in Washington. She looked around the room. "I need to ask Terry if anything is missing or has been moved," she muttered to herself. Next, she sat on a lab stool and dialed the sheriff's office. After several long minutes repeating herself to numerous low level, self-important functionaries, she finally talked to a supervising deputy. She explained that there was a dead body at Buckman Manor, and she needed the sheriff's assistance. She abruptly disconnected as he tried to berate her for not using 911 and thinking a fed had any business investigating a murder in their jurisdiction.

Terry entered and wound around the benches and display cases. "Frank Long has no idea how Sir Edward got onto the island or when. Same goes for the rest of the staff. Sir Edward didn't come to the island while Frank was on duty, at least not through the gate, and no one else saw him. He brought the gate logbook. The other guards didn't log Sir Edward onto the island either."

"I thought that might be the case. Where is Thornwood?"

"Resting in his quarters. This was a big shock for him."

"I bet. I called the sheriff." Virginia wiped her hands on her pantlegs. "Nerves. We're going to have quite a debacle when the deputies get here."

"What did you do?" Terry sat on a stool and held her head and massaged her temples.

"The deputy I finally got to talk to was a self-righteous, condescending idiot. He especially disliked that I didn't just call 911 and wasn't happy that we're feds."

Terry blew an auburn strand of hair from her face. "So, you pissed off the local constabulary while trying to tell them we have a dead body on our hands."

"Yea. And it probably didn't help that I called him a Keystone Cop. I'm not sure if he knew what I meant. The deputies, detectives, and the crime scene people should be along soon."

"I told Frank Long that the sheriff would be coming and to open the gate," Terry added.

"Good. While we wait, go extract and package the DNA samples from the skeleton so we can send them to Tom Mason. We'd better finish it before the sheriff arrives."

Terry's eyes widened. "I'll see what I can extract from the teeth. There might be some viable tissue there. I need to sterilize everything first." She grabbed the tray with extraction tools on it and headed for the skeleton. "I'll get the samples then take them to my room, so the cops won't see them. Hold them off as long as possible." She stopped and closed her eyes. "My stomach doesn't feel good."

"Grab the samples then stay in your room and rest. I'll handle the sheriff," Virginia said.

"As much as my stomach and head like your idea, I've got work to do. Then I'll vamoose. Wait… I'd better come back. You alone with the deputies could be dangerous… for them."

After forty minutes, Virginia and Terry stood in the entranceway to the display and lab room. A man in his forties stomped down the hall toward them. He wore a sport coat, open collar shirt, and jeans, with a gold star, handcuffs, and gun attached to his belt. "Hello, Detective," said Virginia, trying to be polite.

He stopped and glared at Virginia. "I'm Detective Ron Moon. Are you the woman who found the body?"

Terry tensed. "I discovered the body. We identified him as Sir Edward Buckman."

"You what? Did you touch the remains?"

"Only to determine his identity. We also have an old skeleton for you."

"Amateurs," Moon said. "Step aside. I need to see the body." He stopped, turned, and frowned. "Did you say skeleton? Human?"

Virginia held her ground. "First, we are not amateurs. We are federal agents assigned to this case and will be the lead investigators. And yes, we've also got a real, human skeleton."

He stopped. "You two are federal agents?" He stared at them. "Which agency? I need to see some ID."

Virginia pulled her credentials out and showed her badge to him. "Smithsonian Central Security Service."

"Never heard of it." He looked at her ID. "Special Agent Virginia Davies Clark." He turned to Terry. "And who are you?"

"Special Agent, Doctor Terry Sorenson."

"Right. Okay enough with the fake IDs. I'll have to—"

Virginia bristled. "If I wasn't trying so hard to be cooperative right now, you'd be viewing your breakfast on your beat-up cowboy boots."

Detective Moon stiffened. "You can't talk to—"

"Get this straight, Detective," Virginia's features hardened, "*we* are leading this investigation because Washington and Scotland Yard say so, and it has to do with another investigation we are working on."

Moon gave her a blank stare. "You are not Texas law enforcement officers. This is a local matter."

"No. We're federal agents. What I had hoped to do is conduct a joint investigation with the sheriff's office, with the sheriff making the final arrests for the murder. But since this seems to be related to federal offenses, and to our ongoing investigation, we can do it without you." She pointed down the hall. "The exit is that way."

Detective Moon swallowed. "Did you say Scotland Yard?"

Virginia glared at him. "Yep. I'm sure you've heard of it. It's famous and is located in London, England."

"Yeah, I know what it is. I need to call this in. Which agency did you say you worked for? The Smithsonian?" He laughed. "Museum cops? The sheriff is going to love this." Moon pulled out his radio and called the station. Beads of sweat broke out on his forehead after a couple minutes of mostly one way conversation from the other end of the line, then he disconnected.

Moon shook his head as he moved his foot back and forth and mumbled to himself. Then he cracked a smile at Virginia. "Okay. I was out of line. Way out of line. I apologize. The sheriff said Washington has been all over him. He didn't like getting his authority usurped by the feds, and boy is he angry. He verified that you two are real federal agents, your agency is real, and that Scotland Yard has deputized you two. He instructed me to work with you and keep him posted on developments."

Virginia smiled. "I thought the sheriff would have been notified before you got here and told you."

"Didn't happen. Bureaucracy, red tape." Moon chuckled. "Typical. I guess he got the notification just before I called and is still sore. Looks like we're working together."

Virginia nodded. "Are your forensics people here?"

"Downstairs. The Justice of the Peace, he acts as coroner hereabout, is coming as well. I wanted to see what we've got before I called in more support people."

"Smart. You're also going to need a medical examiner. He was killed by Tetrahydrozoline poisoning." Virginia turned. "Follow us, Detective."

Moon raised an eyebrow. "Wait. Eye drops?"

"Yes. They are meant for your eyes. Taking some quantity of it internally can be fatal, as in this case. And before you ask, I've seen it used before."

"Eye drops? For real?"

"Yes. The amount in about four or five small eye drop vials can kill," Virginia said.

They maneuvered around the display cases, shelving, and worktables to the body. Terry pointed. "He's all yours. That's Sir Edward Buckman."

Detective Moon stared. "When did you discover him?"

Virginia glanced at her watch. "About an hour or two ago. We called this in earlier, but the person on the phone at the sheriff's office was… pompous, uncooperative, and an ass."

"That would be O'Malley. He can be a pill," said Moon. "He's almost as bad as me." Moon glanced around. "Looks like pretty tight security. How did someone get in here and kill him? How'd he get poisoned? And how did the killer get away?"

"We're working on it. And on top of that, Sir Edward managed to get onto the island and in here without anyone knowing. He was expected tomorrow."

"I see. May I ask what your investigation is about?"

Virginia nodded. "Some irregularities in artifacts, relics, and art that were donated to the Smithsonian and another museum, antiquities theft and smuggling, a skeleton, a mysterious treasure maybe from the 1100s, and a dragon. Now a murder."

"Harry T. Dragon?" Moon asked.

Virginia smiled. "Silly, we know, but Uncle Sam is interested in him. After all, we work for the Smithsonian."

Moon laughed. "You have your hands full. If you don't mind, I'll call the forensic team up to do their thing. When the JP gets here, he'll call me on my cell. Once he's seen the body, we'll get… Sir Edward out of here and to the medical examiner ASAP. Are you notifying the next of kin?"

"Scotland Yard is doing that in Great Britain, and we'll see if he has anyone else in the US."

"Good. That's a job I don't relish." Moon used his radio to call the crime scene unit up to the room. "This'll take a while. You mentioned something about a skeleton?"

Terry pointed across the room. "Over there on that table. I put him back together and examined the bones. I have pictures and a full report of my findings on my computer. Give me your email address and I'll send you a copy."

Moon raised an eyebrow. "You're a doctor? MD?"

"No, PhD. I'm an archeologist and a forensic anthropologist."

He grinned. "In this case, that's even better." He pulled out his card and handed it to Terry. "Send it to that email, please."

They watched as the CSU people entered and started to work. Moon turned to Terry. "Were you the woman who was attacked by the dragon the other night?"

"Yes. He tried to barbeque me. Now I want to return the favor."

Virginia chuckled. "Two museums want him as well. But first we need to find him."

Moon shrugged his shoulder. "Good luck. You aren't the first to try and catch him."

"We'll catch him. We're good at what we do."

"For your sakes, I hope so."

Terry cleared her throat. "Now that we're done discussing the dragon… would you like to see the skeleton?"

CHAPTER 10

The forensic people moved around the area in their bunny suits, collecting evidence for analysis, as Virginia, Terry, and Detective Moon stepped across the room to a stainless-steel examining table with the skeleton laid out on it.

Terry pointed. "That's the skeleton I found." She picked up her laptop computer from the table and typed frantically. "You now have my report about this man and the photographs."

"Do you think this is related to the murder of Sir Edward?" asked Moon.

"The man whose skeleton is here was killed in the late 1920s to early 30s, so whoever killed him, assuming he was murdered, is most likely dead by now. We really don't know if he was killed or died of natural causes," said Terry. "Is this guy's death related to Sir Edward's? We don't know enough yet to say. With 100 years between the deaths, I'm guessing the deaths are unrelated. But the fact that Sir Edward's body and this skeleton is also here is... interesting."

Moon stepped closer and looked at the skeleton. "I'll take these remains and your findings to the medical examiner. Maybe there's something in a database some place that might help ID him. We can have them do that legwork for us."

Virginia nodded. "He's all yours. You have Sir Edward's body, any evidence found here, the skeleton, and Dr. Sorenson's report and pictures. After you've learned everything you can from them, let us know the findings."

"Right. As soon as the ME's people arrive, I'll have them take Sir Edward and the bones. Is there anything else you'd like my help with at this point?"

"No. Let's just get Sir Edward and this skeleton moved to the ME's morgue. Dr. Sorenson and I will nose around here. We have a lot of unanswered questions to investigate. If we come across anything useful, we'll notify you immediately." Virginia looked across the room at the CSU peo-

Dragon Threads

ple. "Looks like they're wrapping up. Is the JP here yet?"

Moon glanced at his cell phone messages. "He's not coming. Said he's dispatched the ME and will work with them. They should be here momentarily."

Virginia glanced around. "Okay. Dr. Sorenson will remain here with you and the ME's people until everyone is gone. She can answer questions if necessary and maintain security."

Terry nodded. "Okay. What will you be doing?"

"I'll go see James Thornwood IV. There are a couple questions that only he can answer."

Virginia located Thornwood's room on the third floor and knocked on the door. Thornwood opened the door and motioned Virginia inside. They moved to a sitting area with a large window overlooking the grounds to the north.

"How can I help you, Agent Clark? I guess it's going to be a zoo around here with a herd of sheriff's people running around."

Virginia eyed the stately room, which was painted in a dark green, with massive, stained wood features, and a thick burgundy carpet around a king sized, four-poster bed. She grinned at the sight of a stool needed to climb onto the mattress. Paintings and certificates hung on the walls. "The sheriff won't have a herd of people around. There will be a detective coming and going, and the medical examiner and forensics team looking for evidence and taking the body and the bones away, but Dr. Sorenson and I are the lead investigators. The sheriff is backing us up."

Thornwood's face brightened. "That's good news. Is there anything I can do for you?"

Virginia settled back in her chair. "Yes. I noticed you took Sir Edward's demise rather hard. Is it because you worked closely with him for some time or is it something else?"

He took a breath. "Very observant. Yes, there is something else. Do you remember my mentioning Manfred Buckman, the Lord of the Buckman Manor in England?"

Virginia nodded.

"As I told you before, the manor goes back to Anglo-Saxon England, about the time of the Normans, and is a land grant from the king. The estate is quite large and encompasses a huge region, including forests, a few farms, and a small village. Thus, the use of the title Lord by the owner. It is not an honorific peer title; it comes from the estate," Thornwood said. "He is Manfred Buckman, Lord of Buckman Manor.

"Okay, what's the significance?"

"Lord Manfred Buckman is, or was, my great uncle. I was a cousin of Sir Edward's. I knew him quite well. I'm now the last of the family here in the states. I have a cousin in England who is the present Lord of Buckman Manor."

"I see. So, what happens with this place now?"

Thornwood shrugged his shoulder. "According to the documents I've seen, I own it."

Virginia raised an eyebrow. "You own it?"

"I guess so. My lawyer will be calling me back with details." Thornwood's expression grew guarded. "Do you know what killed him? Heart attack maybe?"

Virginia shook her head. "No. He was poisoned."

"Poisoned? Oh God." He swallowed. "Since I inherit the island and all… I know it gives me a motive to kill Sir Edward. But I didn't do it. I had no idea he was even on the island. Anyway, I liked him."

Virginia rose and glanced around the room. "I'm having the IDs of everyone working on this island checked and a background search done by my agency, including you. If there is anything else I should know, now is the time to tell me."

"I was curator of the collection of artifacts, relics, and art in the Buckman collection here. I pointed out some discrepancies to Dr. Sorenson. I think she found a few more."

"What were the discrepancies?"

"Missing items. Also, objects that were of inferior quality substituted for the real articles. Fake documents, paintings, and sculptures. We couldn't figure out how the real ones disappeared."

"How many are we talking about?"

"I found about a half dozen. Dr. Sorenson found a few more. And before you ask, the items were insured for a total of about two million dollars."

"Was the insurance company notified?"

"Not yet. Sir Edward wanted to wait and see what Dr. Sorenson found before action was taken. I think she notified the Smithsonian."

"She did." Virginia went to the window. "Nice view."

Thornwood joined her. "Yes, and if you look that way, you can see the Gulf of Mexico."

A sudden thud sounded, and an indentation in the Lexan window with a few radial cracks appeared near her head. Virginia ducked and yanked Thornwood down. "Get down! Someone is shooting at us."

CHAPTER 11

Virginia and James ducked below the window. Virginia slowly rose to the windowsill and peeked outside. "I don't see anyone. The shot came from the Gulf area."

James took a steadying breath and looked out over the windowsill. "Good thing the windows are bulletproof."

"Why would anyone want to shoot at us or you?"

James staggered to a chair and sat. "I don't know. Sir Edward was murdered, and now someone shoots at us. I don't get it. What have I done? What did Sir Edward do to warrant all this? Why now?"

Virginia looked out the window, then closed the drapes. "I don't know, but we're going to find out." She looked at James. "You look like you could use a drink."

"I have a… stomach condition, and my physician said to moderate my consumption of alcohol. I think this situation overrides that. Let's go to the study downstairs. The bar is fully-equipped, and I plan on remaining there for quite a while."

A frown creased Virginia's forehead. "You go ahead. I need to get Terry and do some investigating."

He looked at her. "You know where to find me if you need me. I hear a grande margarita calling me."

Virginia tilted her head. "No scotch whisky?"

"I need a grande margarita. Never did cotton to whisky."

Virginia returned to the vault. The room was empty except for Terry, sitting on a worktable looking at a notebook. Virginia side-stepped the tables and cabinets, then stood in front of Terry. "Where is everyone?"

"The sheriff's detective, the ME's people, and the forensics folks left with the body and skeleton about ten minutes ago." Terry held up the notebook. "This is one of Sir Edward's record books with some notes about the artifacts here." She placed the book on the table. "You look a little… rattled. What did you do to James?"

"Nothing. While I was with him someone shot at us through the window. It's bulletproof, so we're uninjured, but it was unnerving. James is downstairs in the bar drinking some courage."

Terry shook her head. "What else can go wrong?"

Virginia chuckled. "With us, almost anything. How are you feeling?"

"Tired, and I have a headache."

"Well then, you should rest. I'm going to go do some exploring around the island. Somehow Sir Edward got here without being noticed, and now someone shot at me. I'm not happy about it."

"Sir Edward was also murdered, and the killer got here and left unnoticed." Terry hopped off the table. "I'll go grab some Tylenol and some of the other drugs the doc gave me and meet you by the back door in the kitchen in a couple minutes."

Virginia gave Terry a stern look. "You need to rest, young lady."

"And you need backup. I'll let you do all the heavy lifting, but I'll be a second pair of eyes and another gun."

Virginia sighed. "Okay, but if you feel worse, we're returning."

"Deal. I'll go down, get some meds, and my gun and badge. Meet you in the kitchen."

Watching the area closely, Virginia and Terry walked from the manor house down a flagstone path to the carriage house and selected a two-seat ATV. Virginia scanned the area ahead, then said, "I don't think the shooter is still around. Having missed, and my closing the drapes, he or she knew their presence on the island would be investigated. But keep a sharp eye out anyway." They drove onto the crushed gravel track to the red metal boathouse, unlocked it, and examined the boats stored there. Virginia strolled down the enclosed pier to the sound of creaking of timber. The six small boats and two cabin cruisers that belonged to the manor were all present and on their lifts, out of the water.

Terry climbed onboard each boat and examined the engines and controls. "They're cold. Haven't been used recently." She pointed to a cabin cruiser with fresh paint. "That's the one I used when I was attacked by the dragon." She looked around the area and pointed at the end of the pier. "The rollup doors are closed and locked. If Sir Edward got here by boat, I don't think he came this way."

"You may be right. If he came by boat, he could have landed on a beach or was put ashore by someone."

"Yes," Terry said, "but his shoes and pantlegs were dry. He couldn't have gotten off a boat at the beach onto dry sand. Besides, there was no sign of sand on his shoes."

Virginia turned back and ambled out of the boathouse. "He could have come ashore on the rockier inland side."

"Possible." Terry followed and relocked the boathouse.

They climbed into their ATV and drove across the island and then along the beach on the Gulf side. They could hear the sounds of the surf and the ringing of a bell buoy.

Terry swung the ATV to the right to avoid a turtle. "One problem we have is we don't know when he got here. If he's been here a while, where was he?"

"This isn't getting us anywhere. Let's go back closer to the manor. I'd like to figure out where the person was that shot at James and me." Virginia twisted around and pointed. "That way."

"Okay." Terry said. "How are you going to do that?"

"I took a quick visual from the window, sighting through what would have been a bullet hole to an area where the shooter could have been. It's rough, but once we get close, we may be able to spot something."

"Oh boy, Lucy and Ethel on the case," chuckled Terry.

"You're not old enough to remember *I love Lucy* on TV."

"Remember all the 1940s, 50s and 60s stuff we had for our last case? The *Hidden Threads* case if I correctly recall the name you gave it."

Virginia nodded.

"I read it all and then streamed a few of the TV shows from those periods. Lucy and Ethyl were quite the pair, always in trouble while trying to help."

"Does sound like us." Virginia tightened her seatbelt as Terry turned the ATV around.

The ATV kicked up sand as Terry sped back across the island toward the gulf and the area Virginia had pointed out. She slowed when Virginia waved her hand at a section of the island with scrub brush, small sand dunes, and a few small trees. Virginia had her stop and hopped out. She looked back at the house to gauge her position and the beach, then waved her arm around. "This is the spot. Let's look for clues."

Terry chuckled. "Clues? You sound like Nancy Drew. I think the proper term is evidence."

"Okay, Miss Smarty pants."

Terry joined Virginia, and side by side they marched up and down the area in a grid. Virginia stopped and pointed. "There's a shell casing." She rushed to the bronze casing and carefully picked it up with a small stick. "Looks like a .308 Win. The range is within the capability of the round."

"How does that help? They aren't hard to get."

"You're right." Virginia shook her head. "How did the shooter get here and get away?"

"By using a rigid hulled inflatable boat." Terry stepped a few yards to the water and pointed. "You can see where it was dragged up onto the beach." She took a couple pictures with her phone then walked back to where Virginia was standing. "The house is at least a half mile away and uphill. Seeing you in a window on the third floor and hitting it with one shot is damn good shooting even for a .308 Win. And how did the shooter know you would be in James' room?"

"The shooter wasn't after me. James was the target." Virginia looked up at the sound of raucous caws of seagulls. "This casing isn't tarnished, so it's fairly new."

"Still... someone went to all the trouble to get a .308 Win. rifle, probably with a scope. Someone who has practice shooting at that distance under these slightly windy conditions, who got a boat and came here unnoticed, then waited for someone to appear in that window for one shot in daylight? Shooting a .308 is noisy. Where was security? The shooter had to get off the island quickly and unnoticed. The shooter is a professional or damn lucky."

"The shooter had to know the layout of the building and who was in each room as well. As for the guards, I'll dig into that when we get back," stated Virginia. She pulled a small plastic baggie and a Sharpie from her pocket, placed the cartridge in it and sealed it. She then wrote the date, time, and location it was found and her name and Terry's on the bag.

Terry looked up from a sketch she was making. "Evidence bag?"

"Yes. Maybe Detective Moon can get a useable fingerprint off it." Virginia squinted in the bright light. "What are you doing?"

"Sketching a rough map showing where we found the casing and the boat's landing spot." Terry held up a small yellow electronic device. "Laser distance finder. Every archeologist should carry one. This way I can pinpoint the location for future reference. You can attach it to the bag." Terry handed Virginia the crude but detailed map.

"Thanks. This is great. I'll give this to Detective Moon when we get back."

Terry frowned as she stared at the house in the distance. "Remember when I said Sir. Edward didn't have sand on his shoes and his clothes were dry?"

"Yeah. Why?"

"What if he's been on the island for some time? The house is built like an English manor. There could be secret passages and hidden rooms he'd know about. That could explain how he got into the storage room for the art and antiquities unnoticed."

Virginia turned and stared at the house. "Good call. And James didn't say anything about that."

"He may not know."

"That's something we need to look into and quick." Virginia leaned on the ATV. "While we're out, we could go see the area where your mysterious lights and the dragon came from."

Terry turned back to the ATV. "Nice thought, but can we go back to the house now? My headache is getting worse. I feel like two-day-old road-kill."

CHAPTER 12

Virginia spread out the dragon quilt on the stainless-steel surface of a worktable in the antiquity displays and work room. Sitting, she used a lighted magnifier to examine the brightly colored quilt displaying a green dragon. She twisted it, turned it, folded it, and studied the front, then the backing. Virginia scrutinized the binding, then sat back and stretched. *It's beautiful but I don't see anything unusual from this first examination... well the Virdes dracones de caelo, "There be Green Dragons from the sky," sewn into it is a little off beat. Maybe I'll get more later.*

She switched off the light and started to fold the quilt when she spotted Terry's UV light resting on the toolbox at the back of the table. Virginia nodded slightly. "Why not?" She put on UV safety glasses, picked up the lamp, switched it on, and waved it over the top of the quilt. Virginia's eyes widened as the light revealed a map and some unusual, shaped figures near the dragon's tail. She leaned closer and examined the figures. *This map shows hidden passages and rooms like Terry thought.* She ran her finger along a glowing thread. *The passage to the outside? So, that's how Sir Edward got in here. I need to show this to Terry and find that entrance.*

Virginia glanced at the glowing lines in the section of the quilt below the dragon in the water. *That's an outline of this island.* She ran her fingers across the map contour. *There isn't anything in that area of the island, but what is this?* She leaned closer. *These are some symbols for something.* Jerking up, Virginia reached for her gun at the sound of the massive steel door opening.

Terry slowly shuffled in. "Hi."

"Hi, yourself. You should be resting."

"I was. I got up to use the bathroom. When I glanced out my window, I spotted what appeared to be an old, good sized fishing boat off the coast of the island. Thought you should know." Terry turned, started out of the room, stopped, and said over her shoulder, "It's out in the gulf about where I saw the dragon when it attacked me."

"Fishing boat?" asked Virginia.

Dragon Threads

"Yeah. Maybe it belongs to Brian Kinman and John McDougal, the two guys who impersonated Customs officers like Commodore Haring of the Lost Harbor Yacht Club told us."

Virginia folded the quilt, set it in a cabinet, and locked it. "I'll go check it out."

Terry leaned on the doorframe. "I'm coming along."

"No. You go get some rest. In your condition, you wouldn't be much help, and I'd be worried about you."

"Virginia, you can't go alone."

Virginia took a deep breath and slowly let it out. "How far off the coast of the island is the boat?"

"A half mile to mile. Why?"

Virginia held up her finger. "Hold on a minute." She pulled out her cell phone and dialed. After a brief conversation she disconnected. "Let's go watch the fun."

Terry frowned. "Who did you call?"

"I asked the Coast Guard to investigate the boat for us. After all, we are federal agents."

"They can just board and search a boat?"

"In a way, yes. They can do a marine safety inspection—check documentation, cargo, and licenses—and see what they can flush out. You'd be surprised what they can do. They do law enforcement, port security, conduct coastal patrols for smuggling, and marine animal protection. They run the navigation aids, marine licensing, and other things... like ice breaking."

Terry smiled. "In case you didn't notice, there isn't a lot of ice in the Gulf of Mexico. And you seem to know a lot about the Coast Guard. Old boyfriend?"

"No. If you recall, they helped us in New England, and they rescued Andy and me a couple times. They are the nation's unsung heroes. And I did notice the lack of ice."

"Okay. I'll go back to my room and rest. You can watch the Coast Guard do their thing from your bedroom window. I'll see you at dinner." Terry turned and trundled down the hall.

On the bridge of the fishing boat, *Unicorn*, Brian Kinman clicked the microphone and spoke. "It's me, Brian. We're at the location off Buckman Island as you instructed. But we've got a problem."

"How could there be a problem? It's broad daylight. You are not doing anything illegal," said the voice on the radio. "And watch what you say, this is an open channel. Now what's your difficulty?"

"A Coast Guard cutter just hailed us and said to stop our engines and stand by for boarding. They're going to do a safety and document inspection."

"You are fully licensed and have a right to be where you are. Don't panic. It's probably routine or maybe they're just bored. But make sure the… gear is properly stored. Let me know when they are finished."

"Okay. I'll double check the stuff while the Coast Guard prepares to come aboard. I'll call you after they're finished," replied Brian.

From her bedroom window Virginia watched through binoculars as the Coast Guard cutter approached the big fishing boat and the armed coastguardsmen went aboard. After an hour they returned to the cutter. The fishing boat slowly moved south out into the gulf. *Well now I know the name of the boat. The Unicorn. I'll do a web search for more information later.* Her cell phone rang. She picked it up from the side table and answered it. "This is Virginia."

"Agent Clark. This is Lieutenant Commander Linman, US Coast Guard. I was told to call you after one of our cutters intercepted the *Unicorn*."

"Yes, sir, what did the cutter find?"

"They are a fishing boat and a… sometimes freighter. The captain is John McDougal. The second officer is Brian Kinman. They have a small crew. Their licenses and required documentation are in order." Virginia heard a rustle of paper. "We did find a few safety issues and cited them."

"So, there was nothing suspicious?"

"I didn't say that. The ship has been retrofitted, and there are some peculiar features, but nothing illegal."

"Peculiar features?"

"Yes. There is a moonpool below decks, and a concealable boat ramp with an elaborate hoist system in the stern. She also has a lot of electronics on board. More than just commercial radar and sonar, fish finders, and depth gages, like we'd expect on a ship that size. The radios, the radars, and sonars are almost military grade. They have multiple of each along with satellite phones. Nothing illegal, but not what you'd find on a typical ocean-going fishing boat."

"I see. Thank you for the update," Virginia said. "Did they have any submersibles on board?"

"Submersibles? Let me see what the report says." She heard more paper shuffling. "No mention of any subs. You think the *Unicorn* is being used for illegal activities?"

"Commander, why would they have a moonpool if not to launch underwater vessels and divers? And why would a fishing boat need to do that?" asked Virginia.

"Good question, but having it is not illegal." Commander Linman cleared his throat. "I'll put the *Unicorn* on our watch list."

"Okay, thank you, Commander. Let me know if the *Unicorn* does anything out of the ordinary... whatever that may be." Virginia disconnected. She settled back in her wingchair and stared out the window watching the *Unicorn* move farther out into the Gulf of Mexico. *The Unicorn is no regular fishing boat. I'd bet a Franklin that there are hidden compartments on that ship the Coast Guard doesn't know about, and there are submersibles on her. I need to get onboard the Unicorn for a looksee.* Virginia stared out the window. *The Unicorn was near the area of the map where the strange figures were on the quilt map and where Terry was attacked by the dragon.* She glanced up at the sky. *Those clouds don't look friendly. Inclement weather may be helpful to my snooping around. The island first, then the Unicorn.*

CHAPTER 13

After dinner, Virginia and Terry roared across the scrub-covered sand of the island through salt-laden air in a four-seat ATV.

Virginia turned to Terry. "Are you sure you're all right? Are we going too fast? Should you even be going with me?"

Terry closed her eyes for a moment. "I rested this afternoon. My headache is gone. I'm just tired. But if you think I'm going to let you go out here without me as backup, you're crazy."

"Okay." Virginia steered around a small tree. "Just checking."

"Why are we going out here tonight?" Terry braced herself as Virginia sped across the sand and rocks.

"The *Unicorn* was off the northern part of the island when the Coast Guard stopped her. That's the same area where you saw the mysterious light and met your dragon."

"We're not on the water, and I don't see the light, the dragon, or the *Unicorn*."

"We'll watch for them. But, according to the quilt, people can get to the manor house from the beach undetected. I thought we'd look around."

Terry's head whipped around toward Virginia. "Wait a minute. You found a map in the quilt and somehow forgot to tell me? I didn't see anything when I looked at it."

"I used the UV lamp you had on the workbench, and I found special threads that fluoresced indicating passages from the beach to the manor and also the existence of hidden passages and rooms within the manor."

"So that's how Sir Edward got into the house and the workroom. Do you think James Thornwood knows about them?"

"Hard to tell right now. Let's see what happens with our snooping."

"You're using us as targets?" Terry reached for her oversized bag and pulled out a .357 Magnum with a six-inch barrel. "Good thing I brought this baby and some of the other playthings we've accumulated over the years as well."

Virginia smiled. "You know me so well. By the way, what has that canon of yours got in it?"

"Four full metal jacketed rounds and a couple hollow points."

"Full metal jackets?"

"Okay, so they'll go through a half inch of steel. Don't tell Detective Moon about them."

"I won't ask what else is in there." Virginia pointed ahead. "Just beyond that rise should be our target."

Terry nodded back toward the manor. "Do you hear anything?"

Virginia stopped the ATV and turned off the motor. "Yes. It sounds like a golf cart. Electric motor."

"Yeah, and more than one. How did anyone know we'd be out here?"

"If James was looking for us, he'd know. Maybe it's a security detail. Let's avoid them for now. But we need to find that secret entrance. It's around here someplace."

Terry took a breath, opened her bag again and pulled out two night-vision goggles. "I thought these might be helpful." She handed one to Virginia.

"I always thought the world looked funny through these. Everything's shades of black and green." Virginia slipped the goggles on and looked around. "According to the map, the entrance is over there. Let's go before whoever is coming gets close." They left the ATV, trotted up the sandy slope, then hurried to a rock outcropping. Virginia looked around and spotted an area where the vegetation looked wrong. Fake vegetation looks different from live plants through the googles. "Bingo!" She pushed some scrub brush out of the way exposing a steel door set in concrete. Attached to it was a cypher lock. "Just great. A button combination lock. I hoped we could just open it. Of course, it's a combination lock. A padlock maybe or a deadbolt, but not this." She glanced at Terry. "What else do you have in that bag of gadgets?"

Terry rummaged through her bag. "Some small explosives, a listening device, a nine-millimeter pistol, extra ammunition for my .357 and a box of 9mm, three canisters of the Ketamine-DMSO spray, a can of fluorescent dye, a battery-operated UV lamp and glasses, two flash-bang grenades, a smoke grenade, and a real one. I've got two flare guns with red flares, a Swiss Army knife, and some lip gloss and sunblock."

Virginia gave her a bewildered look. "Lip gloss and sunblock?"

"We're in Texas."

"Good point. Hand me the dye and UV lamp."

"Okay." Terry handed the spray bottle to Virginia.

Virginia sprayed the cypher lock and then turned on the UV light.

Terry peered through the UV glasses. "It stuck more to finger oils on numbers 3, 7, 9 and 0, and they are glowing. Cute trick. Now what?"

Virginia looked closer. "Right. That's well over two hundred possible combinations."

Terry pulled Virginia down. "No golf cart noise this time." She pointed. "There are some strange sounds coming from behind us—to the right and to our left."

"They're trying to flank us." Virginia turned her attention to the locking mechanism. *Rust? The thing has a patina of rust on it. I wonder.* She grabbed the wheel on the door and turned it. The rusted door clicked open and swung back into the dark, dank tunnel. "Inside, quick!" They jumped inside just as a bullet hit the concrete entrance.

Terry ducked, took out a spray bottle and coated the outside wheel with Ketamine-DMSO solution. She stepped inside, slammed the door closed and looked around. With no light inside, her night vision goggles were dark. She whipped them off and turned on the flashlight on her cellphone.

Virginia yanked her goggles off. "Next time you turn on a light, warn me first. That sudden flash of white nearly blinded me."

"Sorry." Terry pointed. "Let's jam this door using that dilapidated pallet, some junk, and a two-by-four."

Virginia dogged the wheel, picked up the board and jammed it into the wheel, so the protruding end of the board was wedged into the raised edge of the door.

Someone outside tried turning the wheel. It didn't budge.

Terry chuckled. "The person who did that will be unconscious for a few hours thanks to the solution of DMSO and Ketamine I put on the wheel."

"The board and your solution will keep them out for a while." Virginia stared into the dark tunnel, and along with Terry, they shined their cell phone flashlights at the walls. Near the door was a light switch. Virginia flicked the switch, and a series of red lightbulbs came on leading down the tunnel.

"Red lights?" Terry asked.

"Doesn't harm your night vision like white lights."

"Okay. Let's see where this goes." Terry walked beside Virginia into the damp tunnel. "At least we didn't encounter my dragon."

"We aren't back at the manor yet. Anything can happen."

CHAPTER 14

Virginia and Terry continued down the tunnel when they heard a loud crack, as the board jammed into the wheel of the metal door broke. Terry glanced over her shoulder. "I think we'll be getting company soon."

Virginia hurried them around a short bend and stopped. "Do you have any wire cutters in that bag of yours?"

"Will a Swiss Army knife work?"

"Yeah. Have any rubber gloves?"

"Ahh… no. But I do have a small roll of duct tape."

"That may work. Hand me the knife and tape." Virginia took the items and wrapped the handle of the knife with a thick layer of tape. She stepped to the side wall where the lights were strung and used the knife to cut the wire. The tunnel was suddenly plunged into darkness.

Terry took the knife and the tape back and stuffed them into her bag. "What did you do that for?"

"Unless our pursuers have lights or cell phones, they are blind."

Using their cell phone lights, Virginia and Terry darted down the tunnel. About a hundred yards further, Terry stopped and shined her light at a side niche. "Door." She wrinkled her nose. "Do you smell something?"

"Yes. It's a solvent of some type." She looked back into the dark tunnel. "Interesting, but not important right now." Virginia stepped to the steel door, grabbed the wheel, twisted it, and quietly and easily pushed the door open. "At least this one is well oiled." She leaned out and peered around. The door was an exit from the tunnel to the rocks and dunes. "Looks clear. Let's get out of here."

Terry followed Virginia out and shut the door. "No way to lock it."

"Spray some more of your Ketamine-DMSO solution on the inside handle then let's go find our ATV."

Terry opened the door and emptied the canister of its contents on the wheel and edge of the door, then reclosed it. "I put enough solution on that door to knock out an elephant. Let's get out of here."

Terry, lugging her oversized bag, followed Virginia across the sand to their ATV. She pointed. "There is our chariot. I don't see anyone around." Terry hopped into the passenger seat as Virginia turned on the motor. "There is hard packed sand along the water's edge, and it is flat. We'll make better time going back if we go that way."

Virginia turned the steering wheel and drove toward the beach.

Terry pointed out at sea. "What the hell is that?"

Virginia stopped the ATV. "Looks like some kind of boat. Get one of your flare guns out and light it up."

Terry rummaged through the bag on the floor between her legs and pulled out an orange flare gun. She aimed it out toward the Gulf and fired. A trail of smoke and fire followed the projectile into the sky, then it exploded. The Gulf of Mexico was illuminated in a reddish glow. A fire engine red cigarette boat's engine roared as it turned away from the coast and raced out to sea and into the darkness.

Virginia shook her head. "Not what I was expecting."

Terry put the empty flare gun back into her bag. "You were expecting something?"

"Your dragon or the *Unicorn.*"

Terry sat quiet for a moment. "My dragon or the *Unicorn?* We found your tunnel. We fought off some armed people. I knocked out a few men pursuing us with the DMSO solution. Got a whiff of some chemicals. We scared off a mysterious cigarette boat. On top of all that you were expecting my dragon or the *Unicorn?*"

Virginia turned the ATV south and drove along the water back toward the manor. "Pretty much. I wanted to verify the tunnel's existence and was hoping for your dragon to make an appearance."

"Now you tell me. I need a drink." Terry glanced around. "I'd be happy if Harry the Dragon never reappeared."

"It's early. Would you like to go into town for your drink?"

"Will I be wearing my little black dress? Going to a nice place or seedy bar? I have a black hoodie for that."

"Well, you will be wearing black. How do you feel about a little night swim?"

Terry stiffened. "I'm not going to sneak aboard the *Unicorn* tonight. No way! I want… no… I need my drink."

"Is that a good idea with your concussion?"

Terry glared at Virginia. "I don't care. Night diving and sneaking aboard the *Unicorn* is definitely *not* good for my condition. I want a large piña colada. Maybe a couple, or three, or four."

Virginia smiled. "Okay. Nice quiet drink it is."

Terry's eyebrow shot up. "Why are you smiling?"

CHAPTER 15

After returning the ATV to the shed, Virginia and Terry walked back to the manor and entered through the kitchen door. They found the chef, Jason, sitting on a stool going over some papers spread out on the countertop. He quickly pushed them together and covered them.

Virginia smiled. "Hi, Jason."

He glanced at the women and straightened. "Good evening, Ms. Virginia, Dr. Terry. Been out looking for Harry the Dragon?"

"Not exactly."

He looked at Terry's large bag she was dragging. "Can I get someone to help you with that bag, Dr. Terry?"

"No. I'll manage. Do you know if James Thornwood is around?"

"He is in Galveston this evening. From what I've been told, he isn't expected back until tomorrow morning."

Virginia leaned against the counter. "Jason, do you know anyone with a red cigarette boat around here?"

Jason sat back in his stool and stared at the hanging copper pots across the room then nodded. "There are several cigarette boats in the harbor, maybe five or six. I think there may be a couple red ones. But one of the red ones has a white stripe down the center."

Terry pulled up another stool and sat. "Any idea who owns them?"

Jason shook his head. "No. But if anyone knows it will be Commodore Haring of the Lost Harbor Yacht Club."

Terry gave him a warm smile. "Thanks, Jason, we'll check it out."

"Did you see a cigarette boat?"

"Yes. Just offshore. Why?"

"Because I overheard one of the guards say he's seen one before, and when he tried to investigate, it shot off into the gulf. Funny thing is, the boat was dark in color and license numbers on the bow were covered."

"Does the boat and the appearance of the dragon have any correlation?" Terry asked.

"I don't know. I don't go out there at night. There are some bogs toward the north end of the island, and at night they can he hazardous. Anyway, I don't want to meet the dragon. I'll stay here in my nice safe kitchen."

Virginia pushed off the counter. "Thanks for the information, Jason. We better be off. See you tomorrow." Virginia led Terry, toting her bag, out of the kitchen and into the library and closed the large, engraved, wooden doors. "Looks like a meeting with the Commodore is in order." She turned when the doors opened.

Jason stepped in and smiled at Terry. "I am sorry, but I forgot to ask. Is there anything I can get you? Drinks? Snacks? You didn't eat much for dinner."

Terry set her bag next to a long, polished oak table and plopped into an upholstered chair. "Yes. Can you make me a large piña colada? Maybe a few?"

"Large piña coladas for a pretty lady are my specialty." He went to the bar near the doorway and mixed Terry's drink. He returned to her carrying a swimming pool-sized glass with the concoction in it and set it in front of Terry. He turned to Virginia. "Anything for you?"

Virginia sat at the table across from Terry and nodded. "Why not? Are you also good with margaritas?"

"My specialty." He returned a few minutes later with a large glass with a salted ring at the lip.

"You seem to have a lot of specialties, Jason. Any others we should know about?"

"Surfing, sailing, cooking, bartending, and shooting."

"Sailing?"

"Yes. I love to sail, and I can handle a power boat, too. I have a Coast Guard OUPV/Six-pack Captain's License."

Terry put down her drink. "Six-pack license? You serve beer onboard?"

"No. It means I can carry up to six paying passengers on the boat."

"Oh." She looked at her empty glass. "That disappeared fast. Any chance of another?"

"Sure." Jason jumped to his feet and hurried back to the bar.

Virginia leaned forward. "He likes you. Maybe you can get him to take us to visit the Commodore and maybe for a boat ride with one of the manor's boats. I think he must know these waters pretty well."

Terry looked at her empty glass then back at Virginia. "We can visit the Commodore ourselves. I think we should do some more scouting around then use his numerous talents for specific tasks when we need them." She looked up at Jason and smiled as he set another piña colada in front of her. "If you would be so kind, Jason, we could use some ham sandwiches, too." She looked at her glass. "Oh, and another of these."

Jason beamed. "How about some grilled ham and cheese sandwiches?" He turned to Virginia. "Another margarita?"

"Sounds good, only just grilled ham sandwiches. No cheese."

"Grilled ham, no cheese. Got it." Jason mixed her drink then left to make their sandwiches.

Terry watched him leave, then leaned toward Virginia. "If I'm here much longer and keep eating his food, I'm not going to fit in my clothes."

"That good?"

Terry sat back with a dreamy look in her eyes. "Oh, yeah."

Virginia pulled out her iPhone and dialed the Coast Guard station. After a quick conversation with an ensign, she disconnected as Jason returned with her drink, the ham sandwiches, and a beer. They ate and engaged in small talk for about fifteen minutes before Jason excused himself and left.

Terry finished her piña colada and sandwich, then asked, "What did you learn from the Coast Guard?"

"Like Jason said, there are five cigarette boats registered in Galveston and the surrounding area," Virginia said. "Two, as far as the ensign knows, are red. Guess who owns them?"

"Our Commodore?"

"Good guess. He has one tied up at the Lost Harbor Yacht Club."

"Who owns the other one?" Terry asked.

"Sir Edward Buckman. But the ownership is being transferred to James Thornwood IV, our host, as soon as Sir Edward's will is filed. Instead of it being here in the boathouse, it's at the Lost Harbor Yacht Club."

"Oh my," Terry said, draining her drink.

"He also said there are reports of a black one in these waters, but the Coast Guard has no information about it. He said it's a ghost boat."

Terry shook her head. "A ghost boat? Just what we need."

"Yeah. I think we should go to my room and do some strategizing. Things are going to unwind fast if we don't have a plan."

Terry sighed. "They're unwinding anyway. Our being here seems to have caused some problems, like the murder of Sir Edward Buckman, the shooting at James, the *Unicorn* and her crew, my encounter with the dragon, and tonight with us being shot at, being chased down a tunnel that isn't supposed to be here, and the smell of solvent in the tunnel. And we now have a mysterious cigarette boat or boats with suspicious connections to people we're supposed to trust. Whatever is going on, the arrival of Sir Edward and us is causing some serious problems for someone. Antiquities theft and smuggling? Drugs?"

"Maybe all three. When we left the tunnel, you asked why I was smiling."

Terry nodded. "I forgot about that. Why were you smiling?"

"I noticed the tunnel we were in was running north, away from the manor. There was a fork just ahead of where you spotted the side door we took to get out. One side continued north and the other toward the manor."

"If that's the case, then the odor we smelled may have to do with the manufacturing of illegal drugs. They could have a drug lab in the no man's land to the north," Terry said.

"Right. It could also be where someone is producing fake antiquities, and the solvent was from coating or cleaning."

"Either way, we need to find out."

"Yes. And I have a plan in mind to do just that."

"Hopefully, your plan won't get us killed." Terry twisted in her chair as the door opened.

Jason entered the library with another tray of sandwiches and placed them on the table. "What won't get you killed?"

CHAPTER 16

Terry, with her legs drawn up under her, sat on the overstuffed chair facing the television in Virginia's room.

Virginia paced. She pointed at the whiteboard she had on a stand in front of the windows. "First, let's address your dragon. What do we know about Harry?"

"It is a mechanical device of some type. It can go in the water. It can fly or at least come out of the water for a limited time. It breathes fire. That part I'm sure of," Terry said, grabbing another sandwich from the tray.

Virginia made notes on the whiteboard "Yes, and it's controlled by someone. We also heard that Harry can sometimes be seen on land."

"Right. So, it must have a home somewhere."

"Maybe an underwater entrance to the tunnel system and a garage for him?" Virginia asked. She took a bite of one of the fresh sandwiches.

Terry nodded. "Makes sense. But why is Harry here in the first place?"

"I think he's used to scare people off and to transport… stuff… from the secret facility to a waiting ship or boat."

"It worked." Terry wrapped her arms around her as she shivered. "I don't want to meet him again."

"That's understandable. Now for the tunnels under the island like the ones we just escaped from. We need to explore them and the ones in the manor."

"How do we go about doing that?"

Virginia pointed at the quilt draped over a chair. "Follow the map in the quilt. Doing this may lead us to the facility either manufacturing drugs, artifacts, or both, and maybe to Harry."

"There is a small problem with your idea."

"What?"

"There are people around who would not like us doing that, as we found out tonight."

"I have an idea."

Terry shook her head. "I was afraid of that."

Virginia stepped to the desk in the corner of her room and returned with an eleven-by-seventeen piece of paper. She used the small round magnets she brought to secure it to the whiteboard. She pointed at the top sketch. "This is a crude map of the secret tunnels and rooms in the manor." Then she indicated the drawing on the lower section. "This crude scribble is the tunnels outside."

Terry uncrossed her legs, rose, and stepped closer to the board. "Where did you get these?"

"The dragon quilt. I have no idea how accurate it is."

Terry leaned closer. "According to this, there are openings or doors in most of the rooms. Have you tried in here?"

"Not yet."

"Want to look now?"

"Yeah." Virginia nodded her head. "After what we just did, I think we should. Anyway, neither of us will sleep well if there is a secret door into our suites. We'll check out this suite and then yours."

"Okay, but I'm still sleeping with my gun under my pillow," Terry added.

"You take the bedroom and I'll check this room."

"How do we do that?"

"If there are tunnels and secret doors, there will be drafts and hollow areas. The doorway will need to be where there are natural seams."

Terry turned and headed for the bedroom. Virginia slowly made her way around the living room, knocking on wall sections. She wet a finger and held it along edges of paneling and nooks. After searching for a half-hour, she stepped into the bedroom. It was empty. Virginia felt her heart race. "Terry!" she called. Virginia jumped when a sound came from a section of wall. She quickly moved to the nightstand and retrieved her pistol. As she turned, the door to her closet opened.

Terry stood there holding clothes back, indicating the opening in the back of the closet. "Found it."

Virginia collapsed onto the bed. "You startled me. Good job. How'd you find it?"

"There is a section of trim near the ceiling. The middle has a small square. I pushed it, and presto… a hidden tunnel."

"Where does it go?"

Terry pointed. "That way. If I had to guess, my suite and closet is the next stop in it."

"Let's go see if you're right." Virginia stood and grabbed a small Maglite from her nightstand drawer. Holding it and her pistol, she headed toward the closet.

"What about our sandwiches?" Terry asked.

"We can finish eating when we get back." Virginia led Terry into the tunnel. They came to another doorway and found the release handle. She pulled it down and stepped aside as the door clicked and swung open a few inches. Holding the flashlight and gun ahead of her, Virginia cautiously entered the space.

She heard Terry behind her. "That's my closet. I think you can lower your weapon."

Virginia stepped back into the tunnel and pulled the door closed. "Let's go back to my suite and figure out how to block it. Then we can do the same for this one."

"Good idea."

They returned to Virginia's suite. After studying the releasing mechanism above the secret door in her closet, Virginia stuck a straightened section of a paperclip into a hole in the side of the square molding, freezing the lock. "Okay, now we need to do this to the hidden door in your closet. I didn't notice any other secret doors into either of our suites. I think we'll be safe for the night."

Terry started for the door, then turned and said, "You'd better back up that map of the tunnels, just in case."

"I've got it photographed on my phone and have extra copies hidden."

"Good."

They went to Terry's suite, locked the hidden passageway door, then went back to Virginia's suite.

Terry sat facing the whiteboard. "When do we start our expedition?"

"Tomorrow, after breakfast. We can go explore the north end of the island. It will be harder to bushwhack us in the daylight." Virginia peered around the whiteboard at the dark landscape. "Bring your assortment of weapons."

"Okay. Now let's finish our sandwiches."

CHAPTER 17

After breakfast the next morning, Virginia and Terry returned to Virginia's suite. They gathered weapons, flashlights, and tools. After putting everything in their backpacks, Terry hastily added a few plastic bottles with various colored liquids inside. Opening the secret door in Virginia's closet, they entered the hidden passageway. They switched on their flashlights and moved down the tunnel to their right. Upon encountering additional doorways, they carefully opened them and discovered a couple more bedrooms. The last door creaked open into the lab Terry had been using.

Terry stepped into the laboratory. "So, this is how Sir Edward got here without being seen. My question is why was he being secretive?"

Virginia frowned. "Good question. At this point we've got more questions than answers. Let's see where the other end of the tunnel goes, and what's along the way."

"Okay." Terry reentered the passageway with Virginia behind her, turned, and closed the door to the lab. They moved back the way they came and then found a narrow passageway that stopped at a wooden ladder affixed to the wall studs. They stood at the ladder when Terry sneezed. "Sorry. Dust."

Virginia shook her head. "I hope no one heard you."

"It is dusty and has a... unique... smell," Terry said.

"Probably the mixed fragrances of gulf cuisine spices and TexMex." Virginia wiped a cobweb from her face. "Shall we continue?"

"Yeah."

Virginia tested the stability of the ladder, then they climbed down to the third floor. "I think James said this floor had more bedrooms and baths. James's room is on this floor."

"Right. Let's see what's on the first floor that has need of secret tunnels." Virginia moved ahead and found the next ladder. They climbed down two more levels to the first floor and followed the passage. "Here is another door. This one is larger than the others."

"Open it. Let's see what's on the other side." Terry watched Virginia slowly crack open the door. It was a large wooden bookshelf that swung into the living room near the fireplace. "I never would have guessed this."

"If you're going to put secret passages in a house this size, might as well have an opening here. Now to find the rest."

They continued in the tunnel, finding doors to the library, study, music room, and butler's pantry in the kitchen. Virginia heard Jason talking on the phone close by and quickly closed the door to the pantry. She leaned against a wall stud. "Looks like almost anyone could go anywhere undetected if he or she knew about the passages."

Terry shined her light past Virginia down the dark tunnel. "This isn't over. We need to know where this tunnel goes. What's your map say?"

Virginia pulled out the copy of the quilt tunnel maps, and holding her penlight in her teeth, she shined it on the paper. "According to this, we're headed into the wren of rooms and under the sand on the island. There is a fork coming up. One way goes toward the beach, the other toward a room, or cave or whatever this blob indicates, and more tunnels and rooms. We haven't stumbled on anyone else using this set of passages so far. I hope our luck holds."

"Me, too. I hope we're back before lunch," Terry said.

"Let's hope we're not *dead* before lunch."

"That would be a pity. Jason is serving fish tacos with fried cod."

"You're worried about not eating fish tacos?"

"A girl has to eat." Terry stepped around Virginia. "Let's go."

They continued walking in the dark, musty tunnel, illuminated by their flashlights, until Virginia stopped them. "That last hundred feet or so was down a slight slope. Now it has leveled off."

Terry squinted into the dark beyond the beam of her flashlight. "I hear something."

Virginia listened, then whispered, "Sounds like something rolling. Maybe a cart or... something. It's getting louder. There isn't any place to hide, so let's backtrack and take a look outside."

"Sounds like a plan. We can come back this way later. Maybe tonight."

"Tonight works. We'll go back and exit the passageway through the living room, then go get an ATV."

"I'm right behind you."

Virginia drove an ATV toward the northern end of the island with Terry next to her, looking at the map from the quilt. Virginia pointed at the location of the doorway to the underground passageway they briefly explored the night before. They continued around a bog and over sand dunes. At the north end of the island and away from view from the manor, she stopped and looked around. "Besides the tunnel we discovered last night, did you see anything of interest?"

Terry put her feet up on the front console. "I saw some outlines in the sand dunes that didn't seem natural. Also, someone is trying to camouflage an exhaust vent about a quarter mile back."

"I noticed that, too. Also, along the shoreline, the color of the water changed a couple times. Again, it didn't seem natural. Let's see what's on the inland waterway side." Virginia started the ATV. They weaved around sand dunes and bogs along the water until nearing the south end of the island. Virginia stopped. "Not much of interest."

"There's a pier closer to the manor. Probably used to bring supplies here."

"They could just drive them over the bridge."

Terry nodded. "Yeah, I guess they could. Then what's it for?"

"Maybe fishing. We can ask about it. Since it is out in the open, our asking would not raise any red flags."

"After our adventure last night, our asking wouldn't generate red flags, they'd generate hurricane warnings." Terry glanced around then pointed. "Let's cut across the island that way and go explore more of the unusually shaped dunes."

Virginia turned the vehicle around and roared across the sand and around bushes and scrub trees to the gulf side, then turned north. Terry pointed as they approached the first misshaped dune. Virginia stopped. She and Terry pulled their backpacks out of the rear seats and strapped them on. They hiked toward the dune. At the base of the gulf side of the hill, Virginia knelt and felt the sand. "Some of this is packed pretty hard." She shuffled through the sand to the base of the hill. She waited as Terry jogged up behind her. They studied the dune for a short time then Virginia thrust her hand against a steep section. "This is man-made. They have stuff like this at Disney World."

Terry moved closer and examined the surface. "Another door. But this one is better hidden than the one we found last night. What do we do now? Knock?"

Virginia chuckled. "Where is that camouflaged exhaust vent you spotted earlier?"

Terry looked around then pointed. "That's it over there on that higher dune."

"Good. Let's go see if there is anything coming out of it we can identify."

They walked to the second dune about two-hundred feet away and climbed to the top. A fake bush partially hid an exhaust pipe. Terry put her hand over the top then shook her head. "Nothing. Whatever this is connected to isn't operating."

Virginia took her backpack off and pulled out three smoke grenades and held one over the pipe. "Nuts. Too big."

"I have an idea," Terry said. She pulled a small vial from her pack, poured some of the liquid on a piece of cloth. Next, she set it on top of the vent then pushed it inside.

Virginia wrinkled her nose. "What is that stuff? It stinks."

"Thioacetamide. It's used in chemical synthesis and as a reagent in labs. It's a sulphur compound and has the odor of rotten eggs."

"I noticed. What are you going to... oh, I get it."

Terry pulled a small plastic battery powered fan from her backpack. "You can never tell when this beauty will come in handy, and I need this at some of the places you send me for the museum. Now for the fun." She positioned the fan above the vent opening and turned it on.

"Think that will be enough?"

"I don't know. Maybe I should have just poured it down the pipe." Terry leaned close to the pipe and put her ear near it. "I'm detecting some movement or something."

"If whoever is inside turns on a blower, we'll get the worst end of things."

Terry picked up a long stick and shoved the cloth further into the pipe. "It may take some time for them to figure out where the smell is coming from. Before they try turning on fans, they may come out to see what's going on. They may not look down the pipe."

"Don't count on that. Let's hide." Virginia looked around. "Nuts. No place to hide. Let's hurry back to the ATV and drive south then turn around. We can wait and see if anyone appears, then drive up like we just got here."

Terry chuckled. "A simple and eloquent solution to a possible problem. I like it. Let's go."

CHAPTER 18

Virginia and Terry scampered down the sand dune and hopped into their ATV. Virginia started it, spun it around, and roared down the sand and behind a low bluff. She stopped, climbed out, hurried to the beach side of the hill, and peered around it. Waves made rhythmic rumble as they washed against the sand. In the distance, they watched as the secret door swung open and three men stepped outside. The men shielded their eyes from the sudden bright sunlight and glanced around, then returned to the tunnel.

Terry dropped heavily onto the sand. "I thought we were going to drive up and say hello."

"Change of plans. Your little stink bomb caused them to look outside but not search for the source of the smell. Looks like it was more of an inconvenience than a nuisance."

Terry ran her finger around in the sand. "That could have been an exhaust pipe and not an intake." She looked at Virginia. "What now?"

Virginia sat beside Terry. "Well, we now know about the passages in the manor and that they go to the tunnels under the island. That means Sir Edward knew that, too."

"We also know they are doing something that involves chemicals, and someplace in there is Harry the Dragon."

"Yes. But we don't know what they are doing and how your dragon gets in and out."

Terry sighed. "We still have a large, customized fishing boat, the *Unicorn*, to examine, and a mysterious red cigarette boat to find."

"What was Sir Edward's involvement in all this... and James Thornwood IV's for that matter?"

Terry rose and dusted off her jeans. "Why don't we go to your room and put all this on your white board, then split up the tasks?"

"Good idea. We may make progress faster. But we don't do anything dangerous unless we are together, agreed?"

Terry nodded. "Agreed."

Virginia climbed to her feet. "I'd better put it all on my computer in a locked file and erase the board, just in case we get snoopy visitors."

"Like us?"

Virginia smiled. "Like us." She climbed into the ATV and started the engine. "I'd better fill Detective Moon in on our discoveries."

After hearing a low rumble, Terry pointed offshore. "Those black clouds don't look friendly and are marching toward us. We'd better high tail it back to the manor." Bolts of harsh starkly white lightning struck downward in the distance like rows of upside-down trees. "I don't want to be out here with that kind of lightning."

Terry got into the ATV, and Virginia quickly drove back to the manor.

In her suite, Virginia sat in front of her laptop with Terry sitting next to her. Virginia tapped the computer. "This was a few inches to the left when we left earlier. Someone has been here and tried to get into it. With the encryption the SCSS put on it they couldn't. But someone tried." Rain pelted the roof. Lightning strobed the room. Virginia glanced at the surge protector her computer was plugged into. "I hope that thing can handle a lightning strike."

"You can always unplug it. It does have a battery."

Virginia laughed. "You're right, but I forgot to plug it in last night and the battery is low. Anyway, I'm going to upload the files to a secure flash drive and hide it. Now let's finish this list then we…" There was a knock at her outer door. "Who is that?"

Terry jumped to her feet. "I'll look." She padded to the door and cautiously opened it.

Jason stood in the hall shifting his weight between his feet. Seeing Terry, he grinned. "Hi."

"Hi, yourself. What can we do for you?"

"I tried your room, but you didn't answer so I thought I'd try here. I wanted to be sure you two were back. This storm is going to be a beaut. And I wanted to let you know lunch will be served in a half hour."

Terry gave him a hopeful expression. "Fish tacos?"

"Yes. Is that okay?"

"Hell yes! I've been looking forward to it. We'll be down in a half hour." She started to close the door then stopped. "Jason, is James back yet?"

"Yes. He's in the library with a gentleman. James will be joining you for lunch."

"Okay. See you shortly." Terry closed the door and hurried to Virginia. "That was Jason. We're having fish tacos for lunch in a half hour and James is back and in the library with someone. Oh, and the storm we saw is heading straight for us and it is a biggie."

Virginia looked up from her computer. "You got all that in… thirty seconds?"

"More like a minute and a half, but yeah."

Virginia saved and locked the file, copied it to the secure flash drive, then shut down her computer. "Our notes are in a password protected file, and the computer needs a password to open it. This flash drive is also password protected." She unplugged the flash drive and reached for a hairbrush. Virginia unscrewed the handle and slipped the drive inside, reassembled the brush, then set it on a side table. "Should be safe enough for now. I guess we should get cleaned up."

Terry raised an eyebrow. "I have an idea. Let's use the passageway and go to the library and see if we can determine who James's guest is and maybe what they are discussing."

Virginia grinned. "Good idea."

"Are you going to call Detective Moon before we go?"

"Probably should. I'll call him now. Then we'll take the secret passageway to the library."

"To save time, why don't you call the detective," Terry said, "and I'll check out the library? I'll meet you in the dining room for lunch."

Virginia nodded and picked up her cell phone. "Good idea. But don't do anything dangerous."

"I won't. I'll take a few playthings with me in case I encounter any… unwanted company."

CHAPTER 19

After talking to Detective Moon, Virginia went to the dining room. Terry sat at the head of the long wooden table eating a fish taco. There were two more on her plate. What looked like iced tea was in a tumbler near her. Virginia smiled as she took a seat at the table. "Looks like you got your fish tacos. Are they good?"

Terry gave her a dreamy expression. "Heavenly. You need to try these. Jason did an excellent job."

Virginia started to rise. "I'll go to the kitchen and see about ordering some."

"No need. I already notified him you are here, and I preordered your lunch."

"You already told him I'm here? How?"

"There is a button under the edge of the table that goes to the kitchen. He said to buzz him when you got here. I just did."

Virginia leaned back in her seat. "Now that lunch is ordered, did you learn anything in the library? Who was James talking to?"

"Commodore Richard Haring of the Lost Harbor Yacht Club. They appeared to be having some sort of disagreement. I couldn't hear much, but the Commodore was not happy."

"Maybe a trip to the yacht club is in order."

Lightning strobed the room. Terry pointed at a window. "You want to go out in that storm? It isn't fit for man or beast."

Virginia nodded, then pulled a piece of paper from her jeans pocket and a pencil from her hair and scribbled a note.

The room may be bugged. We can sweep it later.
After lunch let's go explore the tunnels. We can make
it look like we are going outside then get into the tunnel
system. It may prove interesting.

She slid the note to Terry as Jason entered with Virginia's lunch.

Terry hurriedly hid the note under her plate. After a brief conversation with Jason, she watched him leave. Terry pulled the note out, read it, then said, "Good idea. Now let's enjoy this lunch."

An hour later, Virginia led Terry into the secret passageways in the manor and down to the basement level. Virginia used her penlight to illuminate the crude map of the secret tunnels she copied from the dragon quilt, then pointed at one of the tunnel entrances. "Let's try this way." They proceeded into the tunnel.

"Why this way?" Terry asked, as she shined her flashlight into the dark. "The floor is just compacted dirt. Funny, for being underground on a barrier island I'd expect it to be wet."

"I noticed that, too." Virginia made a face then wet her lips. "Dusty and there's that smell again. As to why this direction, the map says there are two chambers ahead and there's an exit at the water."

"We drove all the way around the island, and I didn't see any openings."

"Maybe it's underwater." Virginia stopped. "Do you hear that?"

Terry stopped and tilted her head, listening. "Yeah. Sounds like some machinery... maybe a forklift?"

"It's just up ahead. We'd better be quiet and go slow."

Without their flashlights, they slowly proceeded ahead with Virginia hugging the left side of the tunnel and Terry on the right, feeling their way along the tunnel. After edging their way for about a mile, they saw light. Inching up behind a large wooden crate, they peered around it. The room was round with a domed ceiling about twelve feet up. Multiple banks of floodlights illuminated the area. Cables ran around the sides of the room. Metal shelves, containing various artifacts, were positioned along the far side. In front of them were eight-foot tables with packing supplies stacked nearby. A desk and nice gun-barrel-metal-colored file cabinets sat alongside. A stenciling machine sat to their right. Various benches, tools, cabinets and shelves, a pottery throwing wheel, and an electric kiln were on the right side. Wood pallets were stacked near the far exit.

"I wonder if Sir Edward knew about this or was killed when he discovered it."

"Good question. I'd love to look at some of those relics," Terry said.

Virginia nodded to their left. "Notice those two men with sidearms. I don't think they'd appreciate you barging in."

"The guy with the crewcut at the table examining that piece of pottery isn't armed. I wonder who he is?"

"I don't think asking for an introduction is in the cards. Something is coming."

They watched as an empty, stocky, electric propelled lift came into the room with another man steering it. He moved it to the side of the exit and stopped. "That's it for now, guys. Let's clean up. I'm buying the drinks at the club."

The man examining the pot looked up. "When is that shipment being picked up?"

"Tomorrow night. The boss wants the drugs shipped tonight though."

"Count me out. I don't like drugs. I'll stick to these pieces of old art."

"There is a bonus if we help package the stuff," said the man by the lift.

"They must be behind schedule. That's when things get dicey." Crew-cut stretched. "I'll see you at the club." He rose and walked down the exit tunnel with the two armed men following.

Terry frowned. "I hope those two gunmen are just leaving and not going to shoot him."

"Me too," Virginia said.

The fellow by the lift pulled a walkie-talkie from his belt and spoke. "The others have left. Want me to go to the lab?"

A staticky voice answered. "Yeah. We could use the help."

"Be right there," he said. The man glanced around the space, turned, and walked down the tunnel.

Terry tightened her auburn ponytail. "Once he's further into the tunnel, I want to look at those artifacts."

Virginia ran her eyes around the room. "I don't see any surveillance cameras, so okay. But make it quick. That drug lab sounds intriguing."

"Intriguing? Sounds dangerous to me." Terry waited a couple minutes, then scampered across the room to the shelves. She carefully picked up two identical gold necklaces and set them on a table. She examined the first one then the second. Picking up a glass bottle from the back of the table she poured a drop of the liquid inside on both pieces. One fizzed a bit. *This one is a copy and pretty good, but gold plate? Not even 24 Karat.* She replaced the bottle and then returned the items to the shelf. She moved to another open shelf and picked up something and examined it. Terry moved to another shelf and scrutinized a couple artifacts. Next, she picked up an earthenware cup, examined it, then started to return it to the shelf when she saw Virginia waving her arms and pointing toward the tunnel the men had gone down. Terry looked around for a place to hide to no avail. She stood at the table as the bald man in a tight, black t-shirt and dark trousers with a pistol strapped to his belt walked in. He spotted Terry and froze. He reached for his gun, then stiffened at the sound of popping. His body spasmed, then he fell. Terry stood looking at his limp form on the floor. Wires protruded from his back. She chuckled. "A taser?"

Virginia stepped from behind the crates, taser gun in hand. "Yes. It's one of the new 20,000 volt models the Smithsonian Central Security Service is now using. He'll be very sore when he wakes up."

"Thanks for the save." Terry pulled a few plastic ties from her pockets. "Let's tie him up so he doesn't return the favor. And we can take his gun."

Virginia looked around the space. "Did you find anything interesting?"

"The jewelry is Aztec and is being copied and probably sold as original. Same with the pottery. That way they can sell copies and either keep the original or sell it, too. But there are some fascinating pieces in this collection."

"Like what?"

Terry's eyes flashed with excitement. "More Mayan and Aztec pottery and jewelry. There are some native North American artifacts of various cultures and even some Viking relics. I found a couple pirate doubloons, flintlock pistols, a blunderbuss… That was kind of expected. There were pirates in these waters. But the interesting thing is the Viking pieces are in a bin labeled Arizona and a few in one labeled Texas. All these artifacts are in the catalog of Sir Edward's. These are the missing items from the collection. Want to call the sheriff?"

Virginia shook her head. "Not yet. We need to catch the people running this operation." Virginia frowned. "Did you say the Viking articles were in bins marked Texas and Arizona?"

"Yep. Maybe they were mislabeled or… we have some new information about the extent of travel of the Vikings. I think we need to look around some more."

Virginia reloaded her taser. "Good idea. Then let's find that drug lab."

Terry knelt next to the sleeping man and sniffed. "Ether. Not good."

"Ether? I thought I smelled acetone."

"You did. They're *making* drugs here someplace, not just importing and distributing." Terry stood and twisted, relieving the stress in her back. "That means these guys are dangerous."

"Right. We need to be more careful."

"Let's check out the drug lab situation."

They crept down the passage in the direction the man had gone. After a few minutes they came to a fork. Terry shined her flashlight at Virginia. "What's your dragon quilt map say about this?"

Virginia unfolded the map, looked at it, then pointed left. "There is another room that way, and this way heads toward the ocean."

"Let's see what's in the room to the right. The smell of chemicals is coming from that direction."

They slinked along toward a light at the end of the tunnel. Drums of chemicals were stashed near the entrance. Virginia pushed one. "Heavy. Full."

Terry grabbed Virginia's shirt and pulled her down into a space between the barrels and the wall. "Company's coming."

CHAPTER 20

Virginia and Terry watched the lab from behind drums of chemicals. Three men entered.

The tallest in a bright red shirt glanced around. "Where did James say the new batch of fentanyl was located?"

The bald man pointed. "Over there. It's wrapped in five hundred capsule packages. He wants three kilos for tonight's delivery. Leave the rest for later."

"Okay." The man in the red shirt moved around chemical lab benches, cabinets, and instrumentation. "Here they are. Three kilos… right?"

"Yeah. Hurry, James is impatient. Wants to get them delivered before those two women at the manor start sniffing around more."

"How's it going out? Car or boat?"

"I think they are going to use the Garrison Fish Company truck. The smell of the fish can sometimes confuse drug dogs."

The man picked up three large bundles and walked toward the exit tunnel. "If this is for tonight, what are we doing with the other stuff?"

The bald man shrugged his shoulder. "I don't know. I guess James will want to get the drugs out of here soon, too. The last thing we need is to have that blonde fed finding all this."

"Does she know about the tunnels and the lab?"

"Yeah. She and that archeologist friend of hers stumbled on an old exit in one of the dunes last night. I don't think she knows what's in here though. But they work for the Smithsonian, so we'll need to move the rest of the drugs soon, just in case."

"How is he going to move them?"

"Use the *Unicorn* or the cigarette boat and get them to the transfer point."

Red shirt shook his head. "Transferring kilos of oxymorphone, oxycodone, amphetamines, fentanyl, Crocodil, and GHB is going to be dangerous. I've spotted the Coast Guard boats closer to shore these past couple days. By the way, what's GHB and Crocodil?"

"GHB is Gamma-hydroxybutyric acid. Crocodil is cheaper alternative to heroin. It's a man-made form of morphine, and about 10 times stronger. It's a combination of several harmful chemicals, including codeine, iodine, gasoline, paint thinner, lighter fluid, and others. Users inject it into the bloodstream, and it has a rapid and brief effect. Sometimes fatal."

"Of course, you'd know that. You're the head tech." Red shirt looked around. "Everything looks okay, everything is turned off, so let's get out of here and then join the others for a couple drinks." He stepped to a cardboard box. "This still has the whiskey James brought?"

"Yes, but it is aged Scottish whiskey."

"Whatever. Let's go." He motioned for the third man to follow. "How come he gets to have a gun?"

"Because I know how to use it and will," said the tall, muscular gunman.

Virginia and Terry watched the men leave then waited a couple minutes before coming out of concealment.

Terry hustled into the drug lab and explored the facility. "Man, this is quite the operation. Very sophisticated." She stopped on the far side of the room. "Here are the drugs they talked about. All dressed up and waiting to go to the dance."

Virginia hurried to Terry's side. "I see what you mean. Wrapped, labeled, and packaged into bundles. Get a load of this. They have a small dragon printed on each bundle and the inscription *Virdes dracones de caelo.* Coincidence?"

Terry examined the small dragon image. "You don't believe in coincidence."

"Did you hear all the different drugs they are about to ship out?"

"Yes, and they're on pallets. Nothing rinky-dink about this operation. We need to do something. We can't let all this get on the streets," Terry said.

"Have any ideas that don't involve a five-alarm fire or us getting killed?"

Terry smiled. "Matter of fact, I do. She walked to a shelf and picked up a reagent bottle. "Oh, this would be good. Let's mix this up."

"What is it?"

Smiling, Terry said, "Phenolphthalein."

"The pH indicator?"

"Yeah. Turns pink in alkaline solutions but is colorless when acidic."

"What are you going to do with that?" Virginia asked.

"Put some in the remaining drug bundles where possible. It's a white solid powder so in most of these bundles it will blend in. Then we dissolve it in water and slip it into that Scottish whiskey."

"Why?"

"It will cause severe diarrhea."

Virginia chuckled. "You're mean."

Terry patted Virginia's arm. "I learned from the best."

"Let's do it." Virginia glanced at the passageway. "We'd better keep a sharp ear out in case someone returns." She took a bottle of the white Phenolphthalein, moved to the bundles of various drugs, made minor slits in the packaging, and then inserted the Phenolphthalein and mixed it. She watched Terry dissolve the chemical in water and carefully add it to the whiskey, leaving little evidence that she had broken the seals on the bottles.

As they finished, the third man with the sidearm strolled into the lab and spotted Virginia. He froze, then drew his weapon and aimed at her. "Keep your hands where I can see them!" A sound caused him to turn and look at the floor as a gray metal container, without the top, spilled a chemical fluid as it rolled closer. Then the blinding flash and explosion caused him to dive for cover. Stunned and temporarily blind, he tried to get up when 20,000 volts of electricity from Virginia's taser made him convulse on the floor.

Terry rushed to him and held a rag over his face. He went limp. She pointed. "For being the big, strong gunman, he wet himself when you shocked him."

Virginia reloaded her taser and frowned. "What the hell did you do?"

"Ether. Very flammable and explosive. And he'll be asleep for quite a while."

"Good job. Grab his gun and let's get out of here."

Terry looked around then raised an eyebrow. "I know we just doctored the drugs, but there're enough volatile chemicals here to burn half of Detroit. Want to just destroy all this now?"

"Detroit? What's with Detroit?"

"Not a very picturesque city anymore. Last time I was there they had potholes big enough to swallow a sports car. There was a road that was half ruts. The city came in and worked on it. Now it is all ruts."

"I'll be sure to not put Detroit on my travel list." Virginia glanced around. "Tempting. Maybe was could just burn the drugs on the pallets."

"The fire would ignite every solvent in the place."

"That could be a good thing. No drugs and no lab." Virginia looked at the man sleeping on the ground. "Okay. Let's drag him out into the tunnel then set this place afire. We'll burn the drugs, and if the lab blows up... oh well."

Terry arched a speculative eyebrow. "I thought you didn't want a five-alarm fire."

"Plans changed."

"Okay." Terry peered at the sleeping gunman. "Dragging him into the tunnel may not be good enough. The gases from the fire will be toxic."

"Let's take him to the antiquities room. That's about a quarter mile away. He can rest with the guy we tied up, and it should be far enough to prevent any poisonous gases reaching it." Virginia went to the fume hoods, switched on the blowers, and opened the vented hoods over the worktables. "That will provide draft to increase the fire but release the gases outside as well as some smoke. The sand dunes will look funny with smoke billowing out into the rain."

After dousing the drugs with acetone, ether, alcohol, and other organic solvents, they set the drugs on fire. Virginia and Terry exited the drug laboratory and headed back to the antiquities room, straining as they lugged the heavy, sleeping gunman. Halfway to the antiquities lab, they heard a woof sound then an explosion.

Terry looked back. "There goes the lab. Every volatile chemical in there just exploded and will burn like a torch. The compressed gas bottles will be next." Another set of explosions racked the tunnel. "There they go. We'd better get a move on. No telling how much of the toxic fumes will reach here."

They dragged the unconscious gunman into the antiquities lab and deposited him near the tied-up man.

Virginia bent down and looked at the man tied to a metal cabinet. "Here's a friend of yours. He wasn't very polite and pulled a gun on us." She smiled at the men. "Oh, there's a fire in the drug room down that tunnel. I hope the fumes don't get this far. They're poisonous."

The man with the plastic zip ties struggled to get free. His eyes were ablaze with hate. "We'll kill you two," he spat.

Virginia patted his head. "If you say so. Have a nice evening. If you're lucky, you'll live to see tomorrow."

Virginia and Terry hiked a mile through the tunnels and passageways to the manor. They climbed the four ladders in the hidden passageways to Virginia's room.

Entering her suite, Virginia pulled out her cell phone and called Detective Moon. After telling him about the fentanyl delivery using the Garrison Fish Company truck, she disconnected. "Now that's in his jurisdiction, and if they find the truck, it's his bust."

"I noticed you didn't let on about the lab or how you came across the information."

"We aren't done with the investigation yet. It keeps expanding. Anyway, we probably destroyed the drug lab and the remaining drugs."

"Well, Detective Moon will be your best friend after tonight," Terry said as she plopped into a chair and pointed through the rain-streaked window at the smoke rising from multiple points on a distant sand dune. "They will know who caused their problems and subdued their men. There was probably a few million dollars in illicit drugs going up in that smoke. There are going to be some very upset bad guys out there, and we are now even bigger targets."

"I agree. While we were burning the lab down, I remembered the men saying James wants this and that. I wonder if that James is also James Thornwood IV, our host." Virginia wiped a strand of blonde hair from her face. "We need to revise our plans. It's now a question of where to start."

Terry leaned back and sighed. "Let's start with what's for dinner."

CHAPTER 21

Virginia and Terry sat at the long wooden table in the dining room with James Thornwood IV sitting at the head of the table.

Jason, the chef, and a middle-aged Hispanic woman served dinner. After placing the main course of beef stew in front of everyone, Jason motioned towards the window overlooking the northern section of the island. "Did you happen to notice the smoke out here?"

Virginia nodded. "It was kinda hard to see at first, but yeah. The wind and rain made it difficult to see what was burning. From our couple of drives around out there earlier I didn't notice anything that would burn like that."

Jason smiled, then turned. "Mr. Thornwood, did you notice it? Should I have notified the fire department?"

James' eyes widened. "Ahh... no, I don't think that was necessary. As Virginia said, there isn't much out there to burn, and it is raining."

Jason nodded. "Yes, sir. I'll leave you all to enjoy your food and will return with apple pie and coffee for dessert later." He and the woman returned to the kitchen.

James sat in silence as he ate. Virginia discussed the missing artifacts she and Terry had listed and that they were going to be searching for them and possible clandestine ways to get them off the island.

James set his fork down. "You, as a federal agents, are mainly concerned about antiquities and artifacts, correct?"

Virginia nodded. "Yes."

"You don't... ahh... investigate other things, do you?"

"Sometimes. If we stumble on something else that is illegal during an investigation, we can handle it or call in the appropriate law enforcement agency and work with them. Why do you ask?"

"Just wondering." He glanced at his watch then pushed his chair back and rose. "If you will excuse me, I have a call to make." James hurried out of the room.

Terry leaned close to Virginia and whispered, "And the plot thickens."

"You're right. I'd love to know who he's calling."

A couple minutes later Jason returned and handed Virginia a slip of paper with a phone number on it. "I thought you'd want to know who James is calling. Here's the number, Agent Clark."

Virginia looked at the number on the slip of paper. "How'd you get this and why are you giving it to me?"

Jason glanced around then pulled a leather case from his pocket and opened it. Inside was a gold DEA badge. "I've been around this part of the coast for a year investigating a possible drug operation. About four months ago I got a job here when the old chef was unfortunately detained by the immigration authorities."

Terry leaned over and looked at the badge. "Any luck with the drugs?"

"I have reason to believe this island is somehow involved, especially when Harry the Dragon makes an appearance. But no, not much in the way of developments. I was hoping to work with you."

Terry leaned back in her chair. "You noticed the smoke outside earlier?"

"Yes, I pointed it out."

"That was a serious drug lab going up in smoke. A few million dollars in drugs went out the vents as smoke and gases. The equipment in there was most likely seriously damaged or destroyed."

Jason's expression turned to a sudden blank look. He swallowed. "Are you serious?"

Terry grinned. "Yep."

Jason glanced around. "How did you find it?"

Virginia leaned forward. "We have a map of sorts of the tunneling system under this island. We followed it."

Lightning strobed the room as Jason slowly sat in a chair. "You... you had... have a map?"

Virginia nodded.

"Did you cause the fire?"

Terry eyed him suspiciously. "We couldn't let all the drugs in the lab get out into the world, and we didn't want to let them make more. We had a little barbeque."

"I've been here four months and never knew anything about any tunnels, much less locate a drug lab," Jason said.

Terry frowned. "Haven't you explored the island? There are rusty iron or steel doors in the sides of some of the dunes."

"I noticed a couple, but I was told they were the leftovers from World War II shore gun emplacements. They were rusted shut. I've spent a lot of time in the kitchen so my excursions around the island are few." Water streamed from drainpipes as Jason sat wide-eyed staring at Terry and Virginia. "You guys have been here for a few days and found the tunnels and wiped out a drug lab. You're good. Did you manage to find out how they get the drugs off the island and who's behind it? James?"

Virginia folded her arms across her ample chest and said in an emotionless voice, "We have some preliminary information, but we can't divulge it yet."

Jason turned as the woman from the kitchen entered. She smiled then asked, "Coffee and pie?"

Terry looked at her plate. "Can you give us… say, ten minutes, to finish then bring it in?"

The woman nodded and left.

Virginia's cell phone rang with the Pirates of the Caribbean theme song ring tone. She pulled it from her pocket. "Hello?" She listened then disconnected. "That was Detective Moon. They found the Garrison Fish Company truck with the three kilos of fentanyl. The fish smell didn't confuse the drug dogs. He's a happy camper tonight."

Jason swallowed. "You tipped the cops about a drug haul?"

Virginia set her phone down. "Yes. We weren't going to let that much fentanyl get into the hands of the distributor."

He swallowed. "Three kilos is a lot. I'm… glad you found it and the lab." He rose from the chair and wiped his hands on his trousers. "I'd better get back to the kitchen." Jason ambled out of the room.

Terry watched him leave. "If he's a DEA agent, I'll… I'll… give up red wine for a week."

Virginia chuckled. "Some sacrifice. You don't drink red wine."

"It's the thought that counts. It seems everyone in these parts has fake government agent badges. Must be a sale on eBay. Remember the two guys from the *Unicorn* who pretended to be custom agents?"

"Yes. But before you convict Jason, I'll call the Smithsonian Central Security Service and get a rundown on him. I'll also ask who owns the phone number Jason gave us."

Terry resumed eating, then a few minutes later looked up as the Hispanic woman entered pushing a stainless-steel cart with coffee and slices of apple pie on it. She set the pie and coffee cups in front of both Virginia and Terry and poured the coffee. She started to push the cart away then stopped. She looked at the main doors and the door to the kitchen and turned. "That phone number Jason gave you is for the Lost Harbor Yacht Club." She then pushed the cart into the kitchen.

Virginia's eyes followed the woman as she went back to the kitchen. "How did she know he gave us a number and which one? Why'd she tell us it was for the yacht club?"

"I don't know. Maybe she doesn't like illegal drugs and wants to help us, or she's another wannabe fed like the others but hasn't had her fake badge delivered yet." Terry took a bite of the pie. "This is good. If nothing else, Jason is a good cook." She looked at the piece of pie. "It would be a shame if he's a crook, too."

Virginia tasted her slice of pie. "I agree." She tipped her head back staring at the ceiling then looked at Terry. "I think we should take Commodore Haring up on his offer of a drink at the yacht club tomorrow, don't you?"

"I could go for a banana daiquiri. And while we're there, are we going to check out cigarette boats?"

"Yes. If it clears up tomorrow, let's take a gander at the *Unicorn* while we are out and about."

"You aren't thinking of going on board, are you?"

"You might want to make that two daiquiris."

CHAPTER 22

Virginia sat in an upholstered wing chair in her room, facing the rain-streaked window, talking to Senior Special Agent Tom Mason at the Smithsonian Central Security Service in Washington, DC. "I need to know if Jason is a real DEA agent and what you can dig up on a Commodore Richard Haring of the Lost Harbor Yacht Club."

She heard Tom typing on a keyboard. "Okay, let's start with Richard Haring of Galveston, TX. He's a member of that yacht club you mentioned, has a Coast Guard ship master's license, divorced five years ago. Retired VP of an investment company. Makes numerous trips to Mexico and islands of the Caribbean. He has also been to Columbia a few times this past year. His travels in the US this year have taken him to LA, Chicago, New York City, and Elisabeth, New Jersey. Wait, throw in Austin and Dallas, Texas, as well. Busy guy. I would be careful around him. His travel itineraries are suspicious."

"Yeah, they are. Does he have any arrests?"

"As long as traffic tickets don't count, no," replied Tom.

"Does he own a boat?"

"Let's see." Tom finessed the keyboard again. "Yes. He owns two and is a part owner in a fishing boat. The… *Unicorn*. Funny name for a boat."

"You don't know the half of it. Every time we turn over a rock another snake slithers out."

"The DEA has him flagged as a person of interest in the drug trade down there. But they haven't been able to find anything to actually link him to drugs. Did that help?"

"Yes. Thanks," Virginia said.

"Oh boy. You're going to hate this," Tom said.

Virginia rolled her neck from side to side to work out the stress kinks. "What am I going to hate?"

"I checked the fingerprints from the glass you sent me. Just got something back."

"Okay. What did you find out?"

"Your cook or chef Jason, is Jason Weathersby."

Virginia frowned. "Sounds English."

"Bingo."

"Is he DEA?"

"No. Born in Phoenix, Arizona. He's a graduate of the *Institut Le Cordon Bleu* in Paris, France. He's worked at high-end restaurants in New York City, LA, and Atlanta. I'm texting you his picture. Is this the same guy?"

Virginia opened the message app and then opened Tom's message. "Yes. It's the same person. And you did a good job with your French on the Cordon Bleu."

"Thanks. I spent a few years in France when I was young."

"Has Jason got any arrests or convictions?"

"Not according to my sources," Tom said.

Virginia frowned. "You said I was going to hate what you told me about Jason. Why? He seems like a nice guy."

"I agree. But there is an issue you should be aware of."

Virginia stiffened. "What's that?"

"Jason's older sister took some meth at a college party a year ago that was spiked with fentanyl. She was in a coma for three weeks before she died. It shook him up pretty hard. Now he's looking for the culprits."

"How did you find all this out?"

"I have my sources. But he managed to trace the drugs to your area of Texas, and possibly Buckman Island. You might want to have a little pow-wow with him. He could be an asset."

"So that's why he left some lucrative jobs to be a chef here."

"Appears so. Good luck and please keep the body count to a reasonable number."

"Okay." There was a knock on Virginia's door. "Thanks Tom. Someone is at my door. I'll call you later with more developments." She disconnected and went to the door. She opened it to find Terry and Jason standing in front of her. Virginia took a breath to slow her racing heart. "Are you two okay?"

Terry led Jason into Virginia's room and took a seat on the couch. Jason sat at the table while Virginia returned to her wing chair. Terry leaned forward. "You're probably wondering why both Jason and I are here."

Virginia clasped her hands in her lap. "I know, you're getting married."

Terry shook her head then glanced at Jason. "I told you she probably already knew."

Jason sat with a puzzled expression. "But we aren't getting married." He turned to Virginia. "We... well I was talking to Doctor... Terry and told her—"

"You traced the drugs and people who killed your sister to this area and possibly this island," Virginia blurted out.

Terry pointed at Virginia. "She's good. And now I don't need to swear off red wine."

Virginia shook her head. "He isn't a DEA agent, you were right. But, like I said before, you don't like red wine."

"Makes sacrifices easier."

Jason rested his arm on the glass tabletop. "How did you find out? I've tried to keep my activity secret."

"From the SCSS. My boss just informed me. Oh, the real DEA thinks Commodore Richard Haring of the Lost Harbor Yacht Club is a person of interest in the drug operation down here on the coast."

Terry wet her lips. "We've got a lot of work to do. And how is all this tied to Jason's sister and Sir Edward's murder and to the old skeleton we found? What's with the art and antiquities thefts?"

Jason rubbed his left eye then said, "Sir Edward arrived sooner than the household thought he would because he had gotten wind about the thefts. He used to come here as a child, and he knew all the undisclosed tunnels and passageways on the island. Kids seem to be better at finding these things than adults. He figured he might be able to find out who was behind the thefts if everyone thought he wasn't here. He wanted to move about stealthily."

"How'd he get on the island?" Terry asked.

"I smuggled him onto the island."

"That actually wouldn't be very hard to do." Virginia rested her head against the high back of the chair. "So, Sir Edward knew you?"

"Yes. We met in Atlanta when he was attending a meeting of Georgia State Archeology Society. I was a chef at the hotel where the meeting was located. He enjoyed the food I was making. We hit it off and communicated. Then when I traced the drugs to this area, I remembered Sir Edward was coming here to do something about his family. So, I contacted him. He didn't approve of illegal drugs. He got me a job here by talking to James. His murder was a surprise to me."

"Did Sir Edward know about the drugs and the lab under the dunes?"

"I don't know." Jason hung his head. "Maybe he stumbled onto it and was killed because of that. I didn't even know the drug lab was here on the island. Was it very big? What did you do?"

"There were six pallets loaded with drugs, wrapped in plastic. If they had a few kilos of each of the drugs the men mentioned on those pallets, we destroyed six million dollars or so in drugs, as well as very expensive fabrication equipment and chemical intermediates."

Jason looked stunned. "How'd you figure the value?"

"Fentanyl alone goes for about $600K per kilo." Virginia said.

"Cocaine can fetch $150K, meth is about $60K per kilo. I'm not sure about the value of GHB, but it isn't a minor amount. There were other drugs mentioned, but these came to mind. Each four-foot by four-foot pallet can hold 3700 pounds, or 1681 or so kilos. Just a pallet of fentanyl alone would be valued at about one million dollars. There were six pallets."

Jason looked stunned. "I... see." He quickly recovered his composure. "You two put a serious dent in the drug traffic around here."

Virginia cracked a smile. "We tried."

Terry sat straight. "Okay, Virginia, what are we going to do now?"

Virginia eyed Jason. "The Smithsonian Central Security Service checked you out, and what they told me agrees with what you said. So, would you like to join our investigation? Remember, you are not a law enforcement officer, and our primary job is the antiquities. But since the drugs seem to be part of all this, we're going after the people behind them, too. I think the drugs and the theft of the antiquities are tied together."

Jason's face brightened. "This is more than I ever hoped for. Yes, I'd love to help you. What do you want me to do?"

Virginia gave him her best boss expression. "You will function as... as a sort of spy in the household and when you go off the island to town. Tip us about anything you learn."

"I can do that."

Terry leaned back. "Who is the woman who brought us our coffee and pie?"

"That's Emma. She works in the kitchen and helps with various cleaning jobs here. Emma's been here for ages. I understand she knew Sir Edward and the owner before him, the late Sir Johnathan Buckman."

Terry nodded. "Any reason to think that Emma may know about the drug lab and the stolen artifacts?"

Jason bit his lip. "I don't think so. She's a long-time resident of the area and a loyal churchgoer. She keeps to herself."

"The Mafia are regulars at Mass every Sunday, too."

Virginia gave Terry a curious expression.

"What? I watched the Godfather. 'Leave the gun, take the cannoli'."

Virginia shook her head. "I had to ask." She leaned back and closed her eyes, then looked at Jason. "Like I said, we can use you as our eyes and ears around here. The staff and locals know you. So, for now, keep us posted on any scuttlebutt you pick up."

Jason sighed. "Okay. If you think I can help doing that, I'm up for it. I was hoping to be a part of the investigation."

"Jason, you are not a law enforcement agent. If you get too deeply involved, it will compromise what we are doing when this goes to court. And you could get hurt or killed. Your being our spy would be an enormous help. We can act on any intelligence you provide."

Dragon Threads

He nodded. "I get it. You're right. I'll see what I can turn up and then let you two do your thing." Jason glanced at his watch. "I'd better get back. They'll miss me in the kitchen." He rose, said good night, and left.

Virginia watched him leave then turned toward Terry. "I hope he is successful at getting us more to go on. We did some damage to the drug operation and know where the antiquities faking department is located. Now I'd like to find their shipping location. And possibly your dragon."

Terry wet her lips. "Another tunnel visit?"

"No. Right now that could prove dangerous. I propose tomorrow we go for a boat ride around the island."

"We already did that. There was nothing to see."

"Yes, but that was at high tide. There is a low tide tomorrow at 10:30."

Terry grinned. "Is it too early to bring a thermos of daiquiris?"

CHAPTER 23

At 10:25 the following morning, Virginia and Terry, dressed in jeans, tight blouses, and baseball caps, motored north two hundred yards off the island's coast in a small cabin cruiser. Their backpacks, lunch cooler, and a large green duffle bag sat on the bench seats inside the main cabin. Virginia could hear the sounds of the surf against the rocks along the cliff as she piloted the boat.

Terry examined the slowly passing coast through binoculars, under a raucous crow of seagulls. A bubble of laughter escaped Terry's lips. "I'll be damned. When we came this way the last time, I didn't notice the land elevation change. There's a rise about a hundred or so feet up. The topography changed slowly." She pointed. "That rock looks like limestone or sedimentary rocks with a lot of dirt."

Virginia turned the boat toward the cliff and picked up her binoculars. "Reminds me of the rocky cliffs of Southern California." She set her field glasses on the console. "See anything of interest yet?"

"Yeah. There's someone on the top of the ridge observing us. He's armed and using binoculars to watch us. Island security maybe?"

"Why would he be stationed there? There is no beach to land a boat."

Terry rose from her seat next to the window and walked out of the cabin to the stern. She examined the cliff as they motored past. "Got it!" shouted Terry.

"Got what?"

"There is an opening at the waterline. Looks like a cave." Terry returned to the cabin and unrolled a map of the island. She marked the spot on it and looked at Virginia. "You thought it might be here, didn't you?"

Virginia nodded. "Yes. How else can they get the drugs out?"

"A submarine maybe or an AUV?"

"A minisub maybe. I don't think they are sophisticated enough to have an AUV, or Autonomous Underwater Vehicle, programed to drive itself out of there into the open ocean and meet up with a ship. It can be done but we're talking some serious money."

Dragon Threads

"I don't think whoever is behind this operation is broke." Terry plopped onto the seat. "Let me guess. We're coming back to explore this cave... soon."

"Did you bring your thermos of daiquiris?"

"Matter of fact I did. I also brought lunch." Terry leaned back against the red vinyl seat. "When are we going on this little outing? Remember, there is a guy on the cliff with a rifle."

"I was thinking about a little diving later tonight. But for now, lunch sounds good."

Terry dug their lunches out of the cooler she brought and spread them out on the Formica covered table, as Virginia moved the boat further north and into a small cove. Terry heard the motor stop and watched as Virginia scanned the area and dropped anchor, then took a seat across from her.

They ate lunch, then sailed back south along the coastline slowing, as they passed the cave now disappearing with the returning high tide. Virginia rubbed her forehead as they continued down the shoreline. "What was in your daiquiris, and lunch for that matter? All of a sudden, I feel woozy." She glanced over her shoulder at Terry, unconscious, with her head on the table, and a spilled drink beside her. "Terry!"

Virginia steeled herself and shoved the throttles all the way forward. She steered them toward the harbor as the boat surged ahead. The boat sent back a choppy wake as it sliced through the water. *I hope we make it before I pass out, too.* Getting weaker, Virginia pulled out her cell phone and speed dialed Detective Moon. When he answered, she told him what they were doing and their present condition. Before Moon could respond, she passed out.

CHAPTER 24

Virginia awoke in the hospital emergency room. She blinked her eyes to clear the fog and glanced around. Wires and tubes were connected to her leading to monitors and bags of fluids suspended from metal poles. She tried to sit up when a nurse entered her draped space.

The nurse smiled. "I see you've rejoined the world. How are you feeling?"

Virginia rubbed her forehead. "Okay. A little woozy. What happened?"

The nurse checked the beeping monitor. "You were drugged. The poison was in your drinks. The paramedics brought you and your friend in. There is a very concerned detective pacing out in the waiting room who is wearing a trench in the floor. He insists on seeing you the minute you are awake."

"Show the gentleman in. And how is Dr. Sorenson?"

"Doctor? She's a medical doctor?"

Virginia chuckled. "No. She's an archeologist and an agent with the Smithsonian Central Security Service."

"So that's why the detective called you both agents. She's doing well. Right now, she's fighting with the ER doctor who wants to admit you two."

"Sounds like her. Okay, let me see Detective Moon."

A minute later Moon stepped next to Virginia's bed. He examined the fluid bags and monitor, then smiled at Virginia. "Hi. How are you doing?"

"Better, thanks. What happened?"

"You were poisoned. I don't think you were supposed to survive. Any idea who did it?"

Virginia struggled to sit up, then looked at Moon. "There's a control around here someplace. Sit me up will you, please?"

Moon located the controls on the side of the bed and raised the back. "Better?"

"Much. The drug or poison was in our drinks?"

"Yep. Enough to bring down an elephant."

Virginia frowned. "Then why are we still alive?"

"You didn't drink enough of it, and you and your partner are young and in good shape. If it had been me, I'd be toast. Where'd you get your beverages?"

"I don't know. Terry got them and lunch."

"I'll talk to her next. What exactly were you two doing?"

"We went for a boat ride."

Moon pulled up a metal chair and sat. "Boat ride, huh? Now that we established you two were on a boat ride, which I already knew, why were you out there on the boat?"

"We went looking for a sea cave. We figured with the underground tunnels and rooms on the island, they had to be taking the drugs and artifacts out by land vehicle or by sea. We know they use land transportation; you caught them with drugs in a van. So, considering they also used an amphibious dragon to scare or kill people, they must have a way of getting things out of there by sea. I think they take them to the *Unicorn* for shipment."

Moon leaned forward. "Underground tunnels and caves on a barrier island?"

"Yes. Terry and I explored part of them. That's how we knew to contact you about the drug shipment in the van."

"What was... how'd you... they store illegal drugs there?"

Virginia nodded. "Someone had a drug lab there to manufacture a variety of drugs."

"Had a lab? Had, like in past tense?"

"Yeah. Terry and I found it. Then there was a mysterious fire. It burned up a few million dollars in drugs ready for shipment and destroyed the lab equipment and intermediary chemicals needed for the fabrication."

"Mysterious fire?"

Virginia nodded.

"So, that was the smoke people saw from the mainland."

"Yes."

"And I suppose you and your friend had nothing to do with the fire?"

Virginia grinned.

Moon glanced down and shook his head. "Heaven help me. Anything else of interest underground on that island?"

"Yep. We also discovered a facility for copying artifacts for sale."

Moon sat back. "Okay. That was a lot to take in. We'll get to the artifact copying later. Now, about this sea cave."

"It's used to get the drugs and artifacts out without being detected, or they have to use land vehicles when absolutely necessary."

"I see." Moon sat in thought for a minute then asked, "Any luck finding it?"

"Yes. And as soon as we get out of here, Terry and I are going exploring."

"Do you have warrants?"

"No. But we are guests on the island and were told to go anywhere we want."

Moon closed his eyes and shook his head. "These are murky legal waters you are entering."

"It's salt water. And what we find may never end up in court."

"Your investigation will hopefully lead to Sir Edward's murderer. You'll need to explain to a court how you found that person, and a defense lawyer will eat you up."

"Court? Who's going to go to court?"

"Huh?"

"A lot of the people we pursue never get to court."

Moon gave her a blank stare. "Where do they go? Do they get off?"

"Well, yeah, some do make it to court and prison. Others end up in the morgue, others... let's say they just disappear... forever."

Moon swallowed. "Oh boy. You and your friend are a little unorthodox."

Virginia smiled. "Absolutely. And we catch over 99% of the crooks we go after. Oh, one more thing. What happened to our weapons and Terry's... utility bag?"

"They are in the trunk of my police car. I'll give them to you when you're discharged from the hospital."

"How about now? Can you help us get out of here?"

Two hours later, Virginia and Terry were wheeled out of the hospital to Moon's waiting police car. Moon drove them to a drug store to fill their prescriptions, then to the manor.

As the women exited the police car, Moon said, "Remember, no midnight swimming or diving tonight. Take it easy tomorrow as well. Doctor's orders." He remotely opened the trunk of his car. "Your things are back there. Help yourselves."

Terry watched Virginia retrieve their guns and her utility bag. Then she leaned into the car. "Got it. Anyway, neither of us are capable of swimming nor diving tonight. I'm all for a shower and some sleep."

"Make sure Virginia follows that thinking."

"I will. Have a good night, Detective, and thanks for the rescue."

"Good night. Keep me in the loop but..."

Terry laughed. "We will, and we'll provide plausible deniability if necessary."

Dragon Threads

"Thank you." Moon drove off into the night.

In her room, Virginia took one of the pills the doctor ordered. Terry took her medicine, too, then sat on a wingchair. "To be safe, I think I'd like to sleep in here tonight. That poison we took was put in our drinks by someone here at the manor."

Virginia nodded. "Go get your gear and move in. Tomorrow, we'll plan our next moves. Right now, I'm going to get some sleep."

At breakfast, in the large dining room that resembled an English castle, James asked, "What happened to you two yesterday? When I got back to the manor, the staff was concerned about you."

Virginia set her coffee cup down. "How did they hear about us being in trouble?"

"You didn't come back from your boat ride, and the Coast Guard brought the boat back. And it was on the TV news. The local news channel had a cameraman and a reporter watching the Coast Guard rescue you. They were also speculating on why the police were stopping anyone from interviewing you at the hospital. Rumors spread quickly. And I saw the police bring you back from the hospital."

"We were poisoned. The doctors at the hospital told us to take it easy for a few days, so we are."

"Pois... poisoned?" James' proper English gentleman posture and bearing came apart. He slumped into his seat and, with a shaking hand, set his teacup down. "Poisoned? How? Who would do that? Are you sure you're okay?"

Terry finished her sausage patty then smiled. "We'll be fine. We're going to do a little sightseeing and shopping today and just rest. As to the who... we got our lunch and drinks from the manor before we went boating." Her appearance turned stone cold. "So, who here wants us dead?"

James swallowed. "I... I don't know. I can't think of anyone. The staff likes you ladies." He regained his composure. "But I will make inquiries and keep you posted."

Terry softened her appearance. "Good. Thank you."

"Where will you be going sightseeing?"

Virginia patted her lips with a cloth napkin. "We thought we'd go to Galveston's historic district, shop on the Strand, and later we'll go to the beach, then we thought we'd stop by the Lost Harbor Yacht Club. Commodore Haring said to go there and check it out, and he'd buy us a drink."

James nodded. "I see. Well, have a good time ladies. I'll see you tonight for dinner. Oh, Jason said he has something special in store for dinner tonight. He thinks Terry will really enjoy it." James pushed back his chair and left the room.

Terry watched him leave. "Jason is cooking something special for me? That's nice." She looked at Virginia. "I wonder what it is."

Virginia leaned closer to Terry. "I told you Jason has a crush on you. Did you notice James almost lost it when I said we were poisoned? Either he's a good actor, or that really startled him. While he's still on the list of suspects, I think we can move him lower on it."

Terry tilted her head. "We have a list of suspects?"

"Yes."

"Who's on it?"

"The captain of the *Unicorn*, John McDougal, his second officer, Brian Kinman. Next is James Thornwood IV, Commodore Richard Haring of the Lost Harbor Yacht Club, and lastly Jason. They're on my computer."

"Don't forget Emma. She helps in the kitchen."

"Right. I'll add Emma."

Terry nodded. "Good. But James stays on the list. Remember what the men in that drug lab said? 'James will want to get the drugs out of here soon'. We don't know if that refers to our James or not. I wouldn't move him too far down on the list just yet."

"Okay, James stays where he is."

Terry slid her chair back, stepped to an ornate sideboard, and peered at the picture above it. "Virginia, take a look at this." When Virginia stepped to the sideboard, Terry pointed. "Look at this painting."

Virginia leaned forward resting her hands on the top of the cupboard and looked at the painting. "What am I looking at?"

"It's a seascape."

"I noticed. Looks like it's off the Texas or Mexican coast in the Gulf of Mexico," Virginia said.

"Right. Something about it bothered me when I first saw it. Now I know what it is." Terry pointed. "Look at the figure painted on the side of that boat."

Virginia squinted at the small boat with a large mast and sail. "It appears to be a figure of a dragon."

"Yes. And it is the same figure that was on the drug bundles we burned up."

Virginia frowned and straightened. "Interesting. It's also like the one on the dragon quilt. That dragon seems to be critical to our investigation. It turns up everywhere. Coincidence?"

"You don't believe in Coincidence."

"I know."

"And it's strange that this painting, with the dragon secreted on it, is hanging here at the manor," Terry said. "Coincidence?"

"Now who's not liking coincidences?" Virginia took a breath. "Let's

Dragon Threads

gather our things and head for Galveston for sightseeing and shopping. Then we'll drop in on the Commodore."

"Your car or mine?"

"Yours. And don't forget your backpack and toys."

"Expecting admirers, are we?"

Virginia's face brightened "Count on it. Let's see who takes an interest in our adventures today. Oh, don't bring any food or drinks from here this time."

CHAPTER 25

After touring the historic district and shopping, Virginia and Terry drove to the beach. They parked on a side street and walked to the seawall. They listened to the sounds of the surf. People of various sizes and ages dotted the sand below. Virginia took in a deep breath, inhaling the smell of salt air. "Nice and relaxing."

"Yes." Terry glanced over her shoulder at a street behind them and chuckled. "Did you get to slip our toy under that car with those two guys who have been following us all day, trying to look like they liked shopping?"

Virginia nodded. "Yes. I did it when you managed to distract them by opening and retying your blouse closed. Their eyes were glued on you. It's sitting under the front seat section. I hope there is enough gas to shoot up through the floorboard and into the car to knock them out. The wind is calm, so now for the fun." Virginia pulled a small black electronic device from her backpack, extended a short antenna, flipped a red lever, and pressed a button. She then turned it off and put it back into her backpack. "If it works like I hope, they should be asleep momentarily."

"You didn't use the fentanyl compound again, did you?"

"No. It's the new propofol compound Washington gave me. They should have been out a few seconds after the stream of gas shot upward and they inhaled it."

"Okay." Terry looked longingly at the beach. "Now what do you have planned?"

"I think it's time to visit the yacht club and Commodore Richard Haring."

"If that's all you want to do, then why did we knock those men out?"

"I'm tired of them being on our tail, we have no idea what their orders are, or who they work for. Are they to just follow us and report or do something else?"

Terry shrugged her shoulder. "We could have asked them."

"Like they would answer."

"We could have been persuasive. I'd like to know who their boss is."

"I'm sure we'll find out soon enough."

Terry looked back in the direction of the car and the sleeping men. "I hope they have a nice nap." She took a breath. "Let's go for a drink at the yacht club."

Terry parked her car in the yacht club parking lot, facing the water. The three-story building had clapboard facades with whitewashed-wood trim. A seagull sat on the wooden railing along the marina, watching them. They slipped their backpacks on and strolled to the entrance. Pushing open the large polished wooden doors with shiny brass anchors as handles, they entered the spacious lobby area, painted a subdued gray with a nautical theme. Model ships and antique navigational instruments were placed around the room. What looked like an eighteenth-century English sextant stood in a glass case. A giant globe dominated the center of the space. The rear glass wall faced the yacht basin and the slips for the members' boats. Large leather sofas and chairs with low tables were strategically placed, with a set near a tall stone fireplace.

Terry turned in a circle. "Nice. I bet the membership costs more than I make in a year."

Virginia nodded. "Probably right. Here comes our first obstacle."

A man in a blue suit approached, holding a tablet computer. He looked them up and down. "Good afternoon, ladies. Are you members?"

Virginia smiled. "No."

"Prospective members? I can get our membership chairman to assist you."

"No again. But Commodore Haring told us to come and see the club and have a drink. Can you point us to the bar?"

"Ahh... you'll have to wait over there by the windows while I call the Commodore."

"No problem, we'll just wander around the lobby, inspecting all the treasures you have on display. Like those Native American Indian baskets, and what appears to be an old Indian birch bark canoe."

"But I must insist that you—"

Virginia gave him a 100-watt smile. "We'll stay here in the lobby. Now be a good boy, and go find the Commodore."

"But... but—"

"Don't blow a gasket. We'll be right here. Now shoo."

"I'll call the Commodore. But those artifacts are expensive, and we don't want them harmed."

Terry took a breath tightening her blouse over her chest. The young man's eyes widened. "Do we look like the type of women who go around hurting other people's property?"

He swallowed. "No. Well... I guess if you stay in the lobby and just look at the displays, that will be all right."

Terry stepped close to him and whispered. "We'll *try* to be good girls."

He blushed as he scurried off toward the office area.

Terry shook her head. "What a pompous ass." She followed Virginia's eyes. "What are you looking at?"

"That canoe on display is an old Seneca canoe. That canoe is not from these parts. It's from western New York State. Same for the baskets and that jewelry." Virginia started walking toward the display, with Terry catching up. "Interesting that it is here."

"Maybe they bought them."

"Maybe. I'd like you to look at them. I could be wrong."

They strolled to the display and examined the baskets and the canoe. Virginia wrinkled her nose. "From my cursory inspection, this canoe seems to be real."

Terry frowned. "The baskets are forgeries. Good ones, but they are not authentic."

They heard footsteps approaching from behind and turned. Virginia smiled. "Commodore! Nice to see you again."

Commodore Haring stopped a few feet from the display. "I see you found one of our more ancient specimens. We have quite a collection of maritime articles, and we rotate them to keep interest in the history of sailing."

Terry pointed at the canoe. "I bet the Senecas aren't members of your yacht club."

Haring's face tightened. "You know their origin?"

"Yes."

"That's amazing. Very few people around here know that's where the canoe is from."

Virginia glanced at it. "It's from the western part of New York State. How'd you get it?"

"One of our members donated it a while back," Haring said.

"May I ask who that member is?"

"That is confidential." Haring motioned toward the doorway next to the glass wall. "Let's step outside onto the deck, and I'll order you ladies a drink."

They proceeded outside onto a redwood-stained wooden wraparound deck with lounge chairs, settees, and tables. Virginia and Terry sat so they could see the doorway and the ramp leading down to the docks and chatted with Haring. When their drinks arrived, he excused himself and told them they were free to explore the yacht club. He then turned and departed.

Terry watched him leave and noticed two men inside standing near the globe. "Those two men by the globe look like the two guys from the car you knocked out. Funny how they managed to locate us here."

"Yes, it is. And take a look at the cigarette boats tied up in the marina. There's even a red one."

"How about that? So, we know where it comes from. But who owns it?"

"Let's see if we can get close enough to get the registration number." Virginia's breathing quickened. She put her hand on Terry's as Terry started to pick up her drink. "Stop!"

Terry gave her a confused look. "What's wrong?"

"Don't drink that." Virginia reached down by her chair and opened her backpack. She removed two small glass bottles, opened them, and poured part of both their drinks into each bottle, then sealed them. She used a Sharpie to label each tube and returned them to her backpack. "I hope the people inside didn't notice that."

"You think they're poisoned?"

"So far, Sir Edward was poisoned with eyedrops. According to Detective Moon, we were given massive doses of Atropabelladonna, commonly known as deadly nightshade. It contains belladonna, atropine, and traces of scopolamine. Obviously not from a drugstore. Now we're nosing around what could be the epicenter of the artifact smuggling operation, and someone doesn't like it."

Terry tilted her head. "How do you know what's in Atropabelladonna?"

"A friend of mine wrote a handbook on poisons, and I have a copy and read it."

"You have strange friends." Terry eyed her drink. "This might be the command center for the drug operation, too, if these are laced with some exotic poison." She looked at the doorway to the lobby. The two men were standing there blocking it. "Shit. I don't think enough of that gas got into the car to knock them out for long. How'd they know we were here?"

"Someone must have called them."

"I think it's time to go." Terry glanced around. "I hope there is a back door. The boat ramp won't help."

"We don't need a back door." Virginia palmed a small air gun and handed it to Terry. "I have mine as well. Let's walk nonchalantly to the door. If they block us or grab us, shoot this into their arm, or body, or whatever body part is convenient. Just be sure to hit bare skin. Then we'll march out the front door."

Terry closed her hand around the small weapon. "What's in it?"

"The propofol compound I used on them earlier. Only this time they won't cause any problems for about another hour or two… or three."

"You are mean."

"No. If I were mean, I'd shoot them up with aconite. Then we would never have to deal with them again."

"I like the aconite better. Let's just get out of here."

They picked up their backpacks, slung them over their shoulders, and strolled to the doorway.

The two men Terry had seen stepped in front of them blocking their exit. The baldheaded man smirked. "Go'n somewhere ladies? You haven't finished your drinks."

Virginia smiled. "We're finished."

"Then give us your cell phones. No pictures allowed," he said.

Virginia looked around. "Where does it say that?"

"I just told you." He held out his hand. "Now hand them over, and you won't get hurt."

He turned his head as Terry spoke. "Oh, have a short nap this afternoon, fellas?"

"That was your doing?" the smaller man asked.

"You looked like you could use some beauty sleep." Terry gave him a curious look. "Need another nap?"

Terry and Virginia pushed the nozzles of their air guns at the men's exposed arms and pulled the triggers. A low popping sound and a swish of gas left the men looking confused. An instant later they tumbled to the floor.

Virginia knelt next to one of the men, felt for a pulse, then called out, "Someone call the paramedics. These men are sick." As a small crowd gathered, Virginia and Terry melted out the front door to their car.

CHAPTER 26

Virginia and Terry hurried to Terry's car and left the yacht club. Taking a roundabout route to observe anyone following them, they drove to the police station and asked for Detective Moon.

After a couple minutes wait, Moon took them to his office. "What are my two lovely feds up to now? You haven't killed anyone have you?"

Virginia sat in a chair opposite Moon's desk and chuckled. "You sound like my boss. But he says keep the body count down."

Moon stared. "You aren't serious."

"Remember I told you that sometimes the bad guys end up in the morgue?"

"Yeah. You also said some disappear forever, too. I thought you were kidding."

Terry leaned back in the chair next to Virginia's and shook her head. "No. We don't kid about things like that."

"Oh. Okay." Moon swallowed. "Do I dare ask? What can I do for you today?"

"We went shopping and sightseeing, then to the Yacht club for the drink Commodore Haring promised." Virginia rummaged through her backpack and withdrew the two small bottles of samples of their drinks from the yacht club. "Can you have these tested for poisons?"

"You think Commodore Haring tried to poison you?"

"We don't know. Maybe he did or someone who works for him did. Or they were just as advertised and not dangerous. We were poisoned once already, and Sir Edward was murdered by a poison. On top of that, we were tailed this morning, and later the same goons tried to stop us from leaving the yacht club before we finished our drinks. They had access to the club, and I don't think they own any yachts. They probably take orders from a member… a senior one at that."

Moon frowned. "This is a new development. I wouldn't have thought there would have been anything like that behavior at the club. How did you get out?"

"We put them to sleep." Virginia saw Moon's eyes widen. "Don't worry, they'll wake up in a few more hours. Now, about the testing of those samples."

"I'll send them to the lab and let you know what they find."

"Thank you. Now, Terry and I need to go over what we have and see how to draw the people behind all this out so they can be arrested."

"If they're running a drug operation and an antiquities fraud scheme, they are dangerous."

"Right. And they tried to fry Terry with a dragon, to say nothing of murder and attempted murder... of us. Now we're pissed." Virginia rose suddenly. "We need to get back to work on the case. Call us with the lab results, and we'll keep you posted of any developments."

Moon sagged in his seat. "Please, don't get killed on my watch. Too damn much paperwork." He smiled. "And I like you two."

They walked out of the police station and to Terry's car. Terry fastened her seatbelt and glanced at Virginia. "Where to? The manor?"

"No. Let's drive to the *Unicorn* first."

"You're not going to try to sneak onboard in broad daylight, are you?"

"Just going to be somewhat obvious, taking clandestine pictures of the ship."

"So, we're kicking the hornet's nest."

"Yes." Virginia clicked her seatbelt in place. "Think about it. While we were at the yacht club, we used our cell cameras to take pictures and photos of the boats. Those two jackasses we knocked out will let the-powers-that-be know we were photographing something. We have also managed to take a number of their operatives down, we found their antiquities duplicating facility, and fried a drug lab and millions of dollars in illegal drugs. Someone has tried to kill us, and now, with us taking pictures of that ship, will get even more upset." She looked around at the parking lot, then thrust her hand forward toward the front window. "Charge!"

Terry started the car and pulled out of the parking lot. "That's what General Custer said at the Little Big Horn."

They drove to the harbor and found the *Unicorn,* then drove two blocks away and located a parking spot near some warehouses. They pulled on their backpacks and strolled down the wharf toward the ship.

Virginia pulled her digital camera from the backpack, while Terry went ahead and scouted good photo spots that would give the best shots of the ship and still be somewhat secretive about it.

Virginia caught up with her at the first location. "Nice. Good shot of the stern area and that man standing watch with a gun." She snapped off a dozen pictures using various zoom settings on the telescopic lens. They hurried to the next spot and continued until they photographed the entire length of the ship and a total of six armed men on the starboard side.

Terry watched, then pointed. "Someone raised an alarm. Another man just came out of the bridge door. Get a shot of him."

Virginia aimed the camera and photographed Captain John McDougal. She kept shooting frames as he shouted orders to his men. Three turned and scurried to the gangplank amidships. Virginia tapped Terry's arm. "Time to go. We're going to have company soon."

They turned and fast-walked toward their car when two burly men stepped out of an alley in front of them. The man wearing a stained khakis short-sleeved shirt and jeans crossed his hairy arms. "Not so fast. There is someone who wants to talk to you."

Terry leaned close to Virginia. "Remember General Custer?"

"Yes, but Custer didn't have a Gatling gun." Virginia frowned at the man. "Give him my regards." She pulled a business card from her pocket and handed it to him. "My number's on this. He can call for an appointment."

He threw the card on the ground. "Turn around. Your escorts are almost here."

"You two do realize this is kidnapping. You can go to prison for this."

"Have to get caught first, honey." He put a hand on the large knife in the scabbard on his belt.

Terry glanced at his hand and frowned. "That's supposed to be some kind of threat?"

He chuckled. "You catch on fast."

Virginia shook her head. "Gentlemen, as much fun as this has been, we're going to be late for our hairdresser appointments. Now, step out of the way, and we can part friends."

The larger of the two men glared at Virginia, grabbed her arm, and squeezed. "I said you're going back to the ship."

With her jaw set harder than granite counters, Virginia reached for his arm, wrapped her fingers around his elbow, and squeezed the hollow spot.

He let out a cry of pain and rose on his toes as Virginia kept rubbing the nerve in his arm. "Stop! Stop!"

The man next to him yanked his knife out, but before he realized what was happening, Terry slammed the butt of a .38 Special down on his hand.

He jerked his hand back, turned toward her, and stared down the barrel of the small silver revolver. "You wouldn't shoot me."

"You have a knife and threatened my friend and me. You're also bigger than me. So, yes, just give me any excuse, and I'll put at least three hollow point bullets into your skull."

He looked at his friend, who Virginia now had dancing on his tiptoes and crying in pain. "How'd she do that to Al?"

Terry chuckled. "Al has a weak spot, and he should never underestimate a lady."

The man swallowed. "Who are you two?"

Terry smiled. "Your friendly neighborhood federal agents. Now drop the knife." The knife clattered to the concrete street. "Now go tell those apes from the ship to go crawl back into the sewer where they came from, and we'll let you go."

He shot an icy look. "Tell your friend to let Al go, and we'll stop the fellas from the ship. They're only a block away now."

"You are in no position to negotiate." Terry stepped back, keeping the gun aimed at him. "We'll release him... Al... when those men return to their ship. Trust me, we can take you and the men from the ship down in a bloody heap and not break a fingernail."

He eyed his partner, now sweating and cringing in pain. "Okay. I believe you. I'll get rid of them." He stepped around Terry and rushed toward the men a half block away.

Terry watched an argument pursue between the man she disarmed and the three men from the ship. Finally, the men returned to the ship.

Virginia released her grip on Al's arm. He sank in a heap on the ground. She leaned over. "I hope you learned a lesson today. Never, ever touch a woman without her permission. Got it?"

He nodded.

"Then have a nice day." Virginia turned to Terry. "Shall we take our leave?"

"By all means." Terry joined Virginia, and they walked back to the car.

They slid into Terry's car and placed the backpacks in the rear seats. Terry chuckled. "Where did you learn that neve pinch?"

"From a friendly med student when I was in grad school."

"How friendly?"

"He was excellent at physical anatomy," Virginia said under her breath.

A bubble of laughter escaped Terry's lips. "I bet he was great with female anatomy."

"An expert," Virginia said in a dreamy voice.

"See, some types of medical training can come in handy in our line of work." Terry pushed the starter button. The engine tried to turn over but failed. She tried again with no success. Then she heard a couple soft clicks. "What the hell?"

Virginia hastily unfastened her seatbelt, reached over the seats, grabbed their backpacks, and with her heart pounding, pushed open her door. "Get out now!"

Terry looked shocked but exited the vehicle and quickly followed Virginia to an alley opening between two brick buildings and turned just as the car exploded.

CHAPTER 27

Terry cringed as she watched the burning rubble. "I liked that car."

The Smithsonian will get you a new one," Virginia said.

Terry raised an eyebrow. "Red with heated leather seats, and XM radio?"

"If you want red and heated leather and XM radio, I'll let Tom at the Smithsonian know he owes you a new car with all that."

Terry gave her a stern expression. "Tell him it has to be new, not used."

"I'll tell him it must be new. Now can we go?" said Virginia.

"I wasn't crazy about the color anyway," Terry mumbled. "Now, besides needing to get a ride, what do you have planned? No more explosions, I hope."

"There may be in the future, but we'll be the ones blowing things up. And I want to find your dragon."

"Harry? Harry the Dragon?" Terry tensed. "Why? Remember I'm not fond of him. He tried to fry me. I like him less than I like alligators."

"I want Harry to pay a visit to the *Unicorn*."

"And if Harry is illusive or uncooperative for a while?"

"Then you and I will sink the *Unicorn*."

Terry leaned against the wall. "Why would we sink the *Unicorn*? We don't know for sure if it is involved with the drug traffic or the antiquity thefts and faking. We can't just go around sinking ships."

"My plan is to get on board and search it. Then, assuming we discover illicit activities, we sabotage it so the Coast Guard is forced to board and find the evidence."

"How does Harry the Dragon fit into your scheme?"

"Your dragon friend can distract the people on board while we search it, or he can attack it. By attacking the *Unicorn*, Harry may give the captain of the ship the idea he's been double-crossed by his co-conspirators and then he will... hopefully act on his own and lead us to the head honcho."

Terry looked down at her backpack by her feet, then back at Virginia.

"For all we know, Harry may be on the *Unicorn* and controlled by the people on the ship."

"True, but I doubt it. I think the dragon is in the sea cave we found. We just have to go get it."

"Just go get it? Just waltz in and borrow it?"

"Something like that."

Terry shook her head. "Okay, how do you propose we do that? Remember the armed guard standing above it? There might be armed guards inside as well. It might be wiser to try and get on board the *Unicorn* and search it first. If we try and go by sea, we may have another problem. When we take a boat out of the manor's boathouse, someone may alert the *Unicorn* or guards in the cave. Going in through the tunnels could be risky, too."

"We don't use a boat from the manor or use the tunnels. We rent a boat."

"So, we rent a boat, wait for high tide, and just motor into it in the dead of night?"

Virginia grinned. "I thought we'd do it in the daytime. No one would expect that."

"In the daytime?" Terry put her hand on Virginia's brow. "No temperature. You feeling okay? You sound a little delusional. Maybe you're dehydrated or the explosion caused a mild concussion. I know the feeling."

"I'm fine."

"You're fine? Not if you want to sail into the cave in the daytime."

Virginia grinned. "I have a plan."

Terry stepped back and eyed her burning car. She listened to the sound of sirens approaching, then frowned at Virginia. "Am I going to like this plan of yours?"

"You have the easy part. And it is less dangerous than what I'll be doing." Virginia noticed the people approaching the burning vehicle.

"I know I'll be sorry for asking, but what's your plan?"

Virginia eyed the car and the growing crowd. "We can wait for the fire department and police to arrive and waste time with them or go investigate the cave. I can explain my plan as we go."

Terry glanced around. "Go where? No car. And those sirens are getting louder. You know we'll have to talk to the police about this at some point."

"Yes, we'll talk to Detective Moon, but not now." Virginia quickly typed on her cell phone then pointed at a coffee shop a block away. "The car rental place is sending someone for us. He's to meet us at that coffee shop. There are two men from the *Unicorn* in that crowd. Time to move." They melted away through the increasing number of people gawking at the flaming car.

Virginia and Terry left the manor two hours later in the rented SUV. They drove to a marina several miles to the south and rented SCUBA equipment and a small cabin cruiser. On board, Virginia changed into her bikini and wetsuit. She checked the dive gear and positioned everything on the starboard side of the boat. She sat inside the cabin while Terry piloted the boat north.

Virginia called to Terry, "How do you like your new bright red bikini?"

"You call this a bikini? It's more like dental floss. It covers nothing. Strippers wear more. Tell me again why I'm the distraction?"

"I'm usually the distraction. This time, I need to do the diving, and you need to distract that guard. Trust me, you'll do fine."

Terry chuckled. "If he has a pulse, this should do it. It would capture their attention even if they were dead. If for some reason this bikini doesn't attract his attention, then what?"

"Improvise."

"Improvise?" She took a breath. "Okay, how long do I need to be his center of attention."

"As long as needed."

"Wonderful." Terry checked the landmarks. "We're coming up on ground, or should I say ocean zero. Get ready."

Virginia climbed into her dive gear and attached a sealed dive bag to her belt. When Terry slowed the boat, Virginia slipped over the side away from shore and disappeared underwater.

CHAPTER 28

Terry cut the engine, set up a stack of cushions at the stern, and lay back. A shiver ran up her spine when she spotted two men on the bluff. The men pulled up cloth folding chairs and watched her through binoculars. *This bright, dental floss sized bikini seems to have gotten their attention.* She picked up a magazine and pretended to read it while observing the two guards. *I hope Virginia hustles. I don't know how I'm going to entertain them for an extended period of time.* She rose and slowly walked into the cabin and returned with a glass of iced tea and sat on the cushions. *I know what'll keep them occupied.* Terry slowly undid the little top, removed it, and waved it at the men. Then, with a satisfying grin, she reclined on the cushions and rested like she was sunning herself.

Virginia swam under the boat and through open sea between it and the shore. She rose close to the surface as she entered the mouth of the cave and swam into the overhead lighted cavern. Inside, she spotted a small outboard motorboat and what appeared to be the famed and mysterious dragon. The mechanical beast was shaped and painted to resemble a storybook dragon. Both were moored to a dock. She swam to the dragon and slowly surfaced, careful to not make a sound. Virginia heard voices at the end of the dock near a tunnel entrance. Virginia pulled herself up and peered up and down the dock. Just to her left was a notch in the cave wall with a couple wooden boxes, a coil of rope, four compressed gas bottles, and a red rolling toolkit. She climbed out of the water and, bending low and out of sight of the men, scurried to the niche and hid. She removed her dive gear and turned. Her heart raced when she saw the trail of water she left on the wooden deck. She looked around and noticed a pipe with a spigot and coiled hose a few feet away, near where she exited the water. She crouched, stepped to the faucet, and turned it on, forming a slow spread of water across the deck where her trail was.

Dragon Threads

Virginia stepped to the dragon and examined it as best she could. *This thing is remotely controlled. Where is the controller?* She noticed some fresh spillage of fuel near a screwed-on pipe. Below was a pipe with a CAUTION: FLAMMABLE sign stenciled on the hull. She maneuvered around the dragon to observe the men. She spied three altogether. One was sitting at a table, screwing a cover on what appeared to be a control box like ones she'd seen computer gamers use, only bigger. The other two were armed and kept shifting their weight from leg to leg, looking at the radios they held. They seemed impatient. Virginia heard bits of the conversation from the radios. The two guards outside were describing the hot topless lady with the mini-string bikini in the boat offshore. The men wanted to take the motorboat out and investigate themselves, but someone on the radio was interfering with their plans.

Virginia moved stealthily down the pier, grabbed a spool of nylon fishing line from the toolbox, and slid into the water. She dropped under water and wound the fishing line around and into the motor's propeller, and then to part of the motor housing. She quietly surfaced, took a breath, and climbed back on the deck. Virginia smiled, water from the spigot was all over, covering her tracks.

Virginia ducked back into the niche as the two armed men came down the wet walkway. She watched as they turned off the water—each accusing the other of leaving it running. Climbing into the boat, one man sat at the bow while the other moved to the stern next to the motor. He fiddled with the shift lever, opened the choke, pumped the gas bulb, then yanked the starter cord. The engine coughed, then fell silent. He yanked again, then again. The engine sputtered to life. As soon as the ropes were untied from the cleats, he shoved the throttle all the way forward. The tinny twenty horsepower engine whined with exertion. The boat surged from the dock and headed out to sea through the low opening. Then the motor seized up, and the boat stopped, midchannel. It wallowed in the water.

Virginia crept toward the other man, who was still working on the control box.

He didn't notice her until she was five feet away. His eyes widened. "Who are you?" A soft burst of air pushed a drug into his neck. He went limp.

Virginia felt his neck for a pulse. Finding the man was still alive, she examined the box he sat on. The label said "Greek antiquities." *He sat his fat rear-end on Greek antiquities? Not cool.* She stood and slid her drug air gun back into the waterproof pouch attached to her belt. She picked up the control box and examined it. *Looks simple enough. I should be...* She heard the men in the boat yelling and talking in their radios. They pulled their sidearms and opened fire. Holding the control box, she dove for the deck. *They'll bring reinforcements. Time to boogie.*

She rose, hunched over, then darted toward the hiding place for her dive gear while bullets pinged off metal boxes and the walls of the cavern. She slipped the dive equipment on and then stopped. *Is this controller waterproof? It doesn't fit in my pouch.* She examined the controller. Finding the on/off switch she turned it on. The dragon responded with a shudder and low rumbling. Virginia dove for cover next to the dragon and untied it. She turned a toggle, and the dragon turned. Next, she pushed the throttle, and Harry the Dragon slowly moved out away from the dock. She increased speed and redirected him toward the cavern entrance and the stranded motorboat. On the left side of the controller was a red button. *I wonder what this does?* She pressed it. A long, hot flame roared from the dragon's mouth and struck the motorboat, causing the fuel to explode. *Nice. I didn't even aim. No more boat. Where are the men?* She looked at the burning remains of the motorboat and spotted the two men swimming toward the side of the tunnel and a narrow stone walkway.

Time to leave and take my new friend with me. Virginia turned the dragon around and brought it back to the dock. She located a foothold, climbed onto the dragon, and directed it out of the cave. Just as she reached the narrow section of the tunnel, one of the men on the walkway on the side of the cave shot at her. The bullet hit the dragon just inches from her right leg. She twisted the toggle, and the dragon rotated. Before he could get off another shot, she pressed the red button and kept Harry turning as hot flames bathed the side of the tunnel in an inferno. Hearing screams, she turned off the fire and rotated the dragon back toward the Gulf of Mexico. Virginia looked ahead and noticed clouds appearing on the horizon. *Just what we don't need, bad weather. Our adversaries will know we have Harry the Dragon, and I don't have a place to hide him. Where does one park a dragon?* She chuckled. *When Terry sees this thing coming out of the cave, she's liable to have a heart attack. I hope she doesn't try to shoot it... and me.*

CHAPTER 29

Virginia steered the dragon out into the gulf. Hanging on to a section of a metal wing, she exited the tunnel into increasing swells. She spotted Terry's boat… and another one about fifteen feet off Terry's port side. A shot rang out as a bullet clipped the dragon's metal ear. She felt her heart start to pound in her chest. Virginia turned and looked up at the hill above her. The guard stood about twenty feet higher on the ridge and a hundred yards away. As he aimed his rifle for another shot, Virginia raised the dragon's head and swung him around. Nudging the dragon forward, Virginia gripped the controller and pressed the red button. The intense flame shot out toward shore as the distance decreased. The guard screamed and stumbled back out of the blaze, on fire.

She turned the dragon toward the two boats and increased speed. The dragon cut through the small swells. She slowed to hear someone talking over a bullhorn.

"Stop where you are, Virginia. We have your friend."

She stopped the dragon. Virginia yelled, "Okay. Now what?"

"You surrender."

"And if I don't?"

"We will kill Dr. Sorenson. It would be a pity. She is quite lovely, but this is business."

Virginia set the dragon moving at slow speed. "I'm coming." She put her diving regulator in her mouth and slid down the back of the dragon into the increasing swells in the Gulf of Mexico.

The three men on the boat watched as the dragon slowly made its way toward them. Terry saw a ripple behind the dragon and stifled a smile. She took a deep breath and moved to the boat's stern.

One of the men, who Terry heard called Mike, grabbed her arm. "Where are you going, honey?"

"Just watching that thing getting closer. It tried to cook me once. I'm not going to stay here if it gets upset again."

He looked at her standing by the gunnel in her minimal bikini, topless. "Trust me, I won't let it harm you. I have plans for you later."

Cold fingers brushed Terry's heart. "I just bet you do."

The boat increased its roll and pitch as the waves increased. One of the men pointed. "Have Virginia change heading, the waves are causing it to change course."

The man with the bullhorn called out. "Change your—"

A dart from a speargun punctured his chest. Startled, he looked down at the rod sticking out of his chest, then dropped the bullhorn and fell over the side into the water.

Terry grabbed Mike's hand holding her arm. She spun around, pulling him toward the gunnel. Then she dropped and yanked on his upper arm. She slammed her foot into the center of his chest, knocking the air out of him, and pushed. She snatched his gun from his belt as he flew over her toward the siderail and pitched into the gulf, gasping for air. Terry watched as he struggled in the water, then he slowly sank beneath the surface.

The remaining man pulled a semiautomatic pistol from his belt and raised it at Terry. Watching her climb to her feet, topless, he hesitated. Then, hearing a noise, he turned his gun to his left and saw Virginia climbing onboard.

Terry swung her arm from behind her back and shot him twice. "Thanks for the gun, Mike." Relief surged through her as the man dropped his pistol, stumbled backwards, and fell over the side. Terry lowered her weapon and smiled at Virginia. "Welcome aboard."

Virginia tumbled onto the deck. "Thanks for the save. I see you attracted quite a fan club."

Terry laughed. "You could say that. But I had everything under control."

Virginia looked around and chuckled. "Yes, you seem to have handled things nicely."

Terry eyed the increasing swells. "What now?"

"First thing we need to do is go get Harry the Dragon. He's motoring out to sea, and I have other plans for him. You might want to get dressed now. Your audience is gone."

"Okay." Terry grabbed a t-shirt and shorts, then returned to the pilot area, turned on the motor, and turned toward Harry. "It's getting rough out here. What are you going to do with the dragon? Take him to the yacht club?"

Virginia removed her diving harness, air tank, and regulator. "Not a bad idea."

"Then what? See if he's a member of the club and has his own slip?"

"I'll call Detective Moon. I'm sure the police will be called anyway when Harry arrives, but better to have someone who knows us there instead of just some patrol officers who haven't been clued in about our activities."

"We will have a lot of explaining to do. What about the *Unicorn*?" Terry's cell phone rang. "I hope this isn't some crank caller trying to sell insurance." She pulled the phone from her backpack. "Dr. Sorenson."

"Doctor, this is Commander Linman, U.S. Coast Guard. We received numerous calls about a dragon spouting fire and gunshots from boats off Buckman Island. I thought you and Virginia might be involved."

"You thought we might be involved?"

"Yes."

"Good guess. Yeah, it's us."

"What's going on? Are you and Virginia safe? Do you need assistance?" Linman asked.

"We're safe." Terry sighed. "We found Harry the Dragon and had an encounter with several unsavory characters who wanted to kill us, but now all is well. Their boat could use a tow since there is no one to drive it now."

"Oh! What happened to them?"

"It would be better if Virginia and I discussed their demise with you in person, along with Detective Moon. Oh, one more thing. The weather is getting worse, and the waves are increasing in size. Can we temporarily park the dragon in your boat basin?"

CHAPTER 30

Two hours later, Virginia and Terry, dressed in shorts and T-shirts, sat on a leather couch in Commander Linman's office at the Coast Guard station. Resting on an upholstered chair was Detective Moon, scribbling in a notebook.

Commander Linman set his phone receiver back in the cradle on his desk and shook his head. "You two are the luckiest women I know. The cutter I sent to get the boat and tow it in searched the area for bodies. None were found. They coordinated their search with the sheriff's deputies on shore and in the cave. They found scorched marks and what could be burnt human remains, but they are basically outlines in the rock. So, no bodies, no crime." He glanced out his window at the boatyard and pointed at the dragon tied to a slip. "Do I want to know how you came about obtaining your friend out there?"

Virginia swallowed. "Not really."

He shook his head. "Okay. What do you want me to do with… it… Harry?"

Terry leaned forward. "Can you keep him… Harry the Dragon… here until we can figure out who owns it and what its part is in all this?"

Linman sighed. "I talked to the Smithsonian while you were on your way here. They have managed to get a federal court to issue a hold on it, so yes, he can stay here."

Detective Moon looked up from his notes. "So far, no one has reported a green dragon being stolen, so I don't care where you got it. Now, how is all this tied to Sir Edward's murder?"

Virginia turned to Terry. "Doctor Sorenson has some ideas. I'll let her explain."

Terry stood and walked to the window, looked at the rain pelting the window, turned, and leaned against the sill. "Let's review what we know. Sir Edward arrived at Buckman Island unannounced, but he had help. He knew his way around through secret passages in the walls. From the traces of dirt and sand on his trousers and shoes, we know he knew about the caves and tunnels under the island. Did he know about the drug operation? From what we have learned, we doubt it. It is more likely he stumbled upon the antiquities racket that was being conducted."

"How about the skeleton?" Moon asked.

"I told you all I knew about him. How about you? Any luck?"

"Some. I had our lab folks go over it with a fine-toothed comb. Nothing. But I asked a forensic anthropologist from Texas State to look at him. The expert agreed with your findings but found the skeleton had another illness that is not common here, but is in England. So, our skeleton was sick and managed to make his way here. This doesn't help us much though," Moon said.

Thunder roared as Terry asked, "Did you notice the ring he had?"

"Yeah. It's in the evidence locker. It's twenty karat gold. It had a good sized green gem of some type in it, too."

"And the inscription? Did you translate it?"

"Ahh… no."

"It says, *Virdes dracones de caelo … Henry Curtmantle. The great save*."

"What does *Virdes dracones de caelo* mean?" Moon asked. "And who's Henry Curtmantle?"

"He was King Henry II. Ruled from about 1154 to 1189. He died at fifty-six. He created the House of Buckman and made the first Lord Buckman a Baron. The 'save' the King mentioned had something to do with a dragon," Terry said. "Oh, *Virdes dracones de caelo* means… there be green dragons from the sky."

"Nice to know, Doctor, but what does that have to do with Sir Edward's murder."

"The skeleton was a Buckman and an important one."

Virginia cleared her throat. "The skeleton died between 1919 and the 1930s. He couldn't be the guy who helped a king in the 1100s."

"No. He was a direct descendant."

"But he was dead long before Sir Edward got here," Moon said. "We don't know exactly when he got here."

"Right. But when Edward found the skeleton and what was going on, someone killed him. Someone he knew."

Virginia sat straighter. "So, Sir Edward was not just a baronet, but also a Baron, and entitled to use Lord as a title. *Virdes dracones de caelo* could be like a family motto now. I wonder if Sir Edward knew this before he got here or learned it from the skeleton."

Terry smiled. "I think your supposition is correct, too."

"That gives a motive to a certain relative."

Commander Linman shook his head. "What does that have to do with the… mechanical dragon I have tied to a pier?"

"*Virdes dracones de caelo*. Someone is using that saying as a means to identify themselves to others. The dragon tied up out there was an attempt to ward off unwanted attention until the criminals are finished. It perpetuated the myth in someone's mind," Terry said.

"I'll have the dragon examined. Maybe we can figure out who built it from the components," Linman said.

Terry turned and stared at the dragon rocking at its moorings in the rain. "I think we can use the term *Virdes dracones de caelo* and what we know to flush out the people behind this. We have the quilt with *Virdes dracones de caelo* on it."

"It's also on the fireplace mantel," Virginia said.

"The dragon on the quilt is green," Terry noted. "So is Harry. Someone keeping tradition in the family?"

"Oh boy. Who are you two going to kill now?" Moon asked.

"No one, yet." Virginia leaned back in her chair. "We've got a manor on an island in the Gulf of Texas with concrete tunnels and a few natural rock caves. We have a destroyed drug operation, and a facility to copy artifacts and sell them. We've also got a dead baronet and a skeleton related to him. The skeleton has a ring with a green gem that obviously is not jade or another common gemstone. Then there is the green dragon on the quilt with *Virdes dracones de caelo* on it, and the same Latin statement is carved into the mantle at the manor. Lastly, we have Harry."

"What's all this got to do with little green men from space?"

"Not little green men, Detective, but a green gem," responded Terry. "I just checked on the Internet on my phone, and found there was a spectacular meteor shower when King Henry II ruled in the year 1192. You can have the stone in the ring from the skeleton checked, Detective, but I'll bet it's moldavite."

"This is really getting interesting," said Commander Linman, his eyes wide. He templed his fingers and leaned forward. "A couple questions, if I may. Number one, what is moldavite, and how is this important?"

Terry smiled. "Moldavite is made up of... well... alien green crystals. I mean, they came from outer space. They are the remains of a meteor that crashed into the planet. There are ancient reports in part of England, where the original Buckman Manor and estate is located, that a fiery green dragon flew across the sky and fell on the estate. Being a product of extraterrestrial activity, it would have caused social anxiety. You know, something with mystical powers or a warning from heaven or some other reaction. The green semiprecious stones are in quite limited supply."

"That ring most likely has a piece of the stone in it," Virginia stated. "Now, since there are a lot of ancient artifacts from the Buckman estate in England here, the saying *Virdes dracones de caelo* in a number of places, and a lot of interest in keeping people at bay, it seems logical that there is a larger sample of moldavite on Buckman Island, and it may well have been carved into the shape of a dragon. The historical significance is enormous, to say nothing of the value."

"Valuable enough for murder?" asked Moon.

Virginia nodded. "Yes."

CHAPTER 31

Virginia and Terry returned to the manor on Buckman Island. After changing into cocktail dresses, they stood on the covered veranda outside the dining room, as rain pelted the roof. They sipped their strawberry daiquiris and listening to the roar of the pounding surf on the beach below.

"I'm glad Detective Moon didn't ask how I obtained Harry the Dragon," Virginia said.

Terry raised an eyebrow. "Me, too. That could have been interesting, and we could be in jail."

"I figured, since we are both guests here, and Harry obviously belongs to the manor, then I just borrowed him."

"I'm not sure how the law would view your cavalier reasoning, but it works for me. Given the damage we've done to the drug people hereabout, I think the pressure cooker is about to blow up." Terry sighed, then ran her hand down her dress. "This is short and low cut, but next to that red dental floss bikini you talked me into, this feels more like a Hawaiian muumuu and could be worn to church on Sunday."

Virginia laughed. "Dental floss-sized bikini, you wish… you had even less on most of the day, and I'm glad you were so attired. You being topless saved me when that gunman hesitated and couldn't take his eyes off you, and you shot him before he shot me."

"Okay, it was a good idea. But, to change the subject, do you have any idea where the green moldavite dragon statue is?"

I think it may be in a couple places. In the… the artifact duplication cave, or here in the manor. It's probably hidden here inside the manor."

"It's way too valuable to leave out on a shelf or table," noted Terry.

Virginia's eyes widened. A slow grin spread across her face. "You are brilliant, Dr. Sorenson."

Terry set her glass on a black iron table and grinned. "Of course, I am. Why? What did I say?"

"You figured out where the dragon is."

Terry frowned. "Oh. Where did I say it is?"

Virginia turned and walked inside the dining room and set her glass on the table. "You said, 'it's too valuable to leave out on a shelf or table'."

"Yeah."

"As you know, my husband, Andy, is an amateur magician. He has said if you want to hide something, place it in plain sight. The green dragon is hidden in plain sight here in the manor."

Terry looked around. "So, we have to just go look for it."

"Right."

"This is a big place."

"Remember, it will be in a conspicuous location."

"How about the killer? And, who's the drug kingpin?" Terry asked.

"Oh, I know who's behind the murder, the antiquities fraud and thefts, and I know who the drug leader is. Now all I need is the proof."

"That helps. The courts like evidence." Terry moved to the long table as dinner was brought in, followed by James Thornwood IV.

James nodded toward the women. "Good evening, ladies. I hear you had an interesting day."

Virginia smirked. "You might say that."

"I understand you found Harry the Dragon and captured it."

"Yes. And the Coast Guard has custody of it under a federal court order."

"I see." He gestured with a wave. "Shall we take our seats and dine?"

In the galley of the *Unicorn,* Brian Kinman and John McDougal, smoking cigarettes, sat across a marred, wooden table from Commodore Richard Haring, dressed in tan slacks and a blue blazer... the nautical attire of the Lost Harbor Yacht Club.

Brian stamped out his cigarette in an old, chipped, Harrah's club casino ashtray. "Okay, Commodore Haring, what do we do now?"

"Those two federal agents, Virginia Davies Clark and Dr. Terry Sorenson, have become flies in our ointment. At least you were not visited by those two women. They've been to the yacht club and into the tunnels on Buckman Island."

"They were snooping around the other day, and we sent a couple of guys to dissuade them."

"How'd that turn out?" Haring asked.

"It seems someone else got to them first, and things didn't go well. One of the other guys told our crew to beat it. He said Mrs. Clark and Dr. Sorenson were causing his friend a lot of pain and would critically hurt him if they continued towards them. My crewman looked where his buddy was, and whatever the women were doing to his friend looked extremely painful.

These guys were big, but they were afraid of those two ladies. So, my men came back to the *Unicorn*. The women haven't been back," Brian said.

John took a drag on his cigarette and slowly blew out the smoke, then coughed. "These things are going to kill me. I heard the women got the big dragon."

Haring nodded. "That is correct."

"How are we going to keep folks from interfering without it? This is going to complicate our mission. May cost you more."

Commodore Haring adjusted his tie. "The way I figure it is, we do not need said dragon anymore. Those two women are federal agents, and they're good. The two of them found and destroyed the drug lab in the cave on Buckman Island and burned up over six million dollars in product. They have killed or seriously wounded several of our men. Shortly after they arrived, the sheriff intercepted a large drug shipment that was being delivered in a van. I think the women were behind that, too. Those two have put a lot of hurt in our operation. Staying the course does not seem prudent for our continued freedom."

"Meaning?"

"We pack up shop and get out of Dodge," Haring said. He watched the overhead light fixture sway. "Even in the harbor, things are getting rough."

Brian slammed his fist on the table. "Look, Haring, we've got a good operation going here. Good customers and heavy commitments. You agreed to supply us what we needed, and we agreed to do the logistics."

"We have had a couple serious setbacks, now we need to reassess—" Haring tried to say.

"We've still got the last half ton of the new, stronger Meth and fentanyl in the hidden hold of the *Unicorn* to deliver," Brian stated. "This makes us nervous. Things are getting hot, and I don't like it. First the lab is burned up, you lost millions in product, which will cost you and us money and customers, and now our dragon is in the custody of the government."

"You are correct, Brian," Haring said. "We have also lost a few men since the women arrived, too. They've done more damage than the DEA ever did. And they aren't DEA agents. But we need to think this through. I say we regroup and—"

"Haring... our deal isn't over," John said. "We have commitments for delivery of the new stronger stuff, which means you have commitments. You aren't backing out."

Haring glanced around through the cigarette haze at the ill-kept galley with stains, cigarette burned spots on the table and counter tops, yellowing linoleum on the floor, and dirty dishes—with unidentifiable materials clinging to them—stacked in the sink for who knew how long. "Gentlemen, I didn't say I wanted to back out. I said we move the operation, not shut it down. We take a short holiday, find another port, then resume operations."

He shuddered as the smell of burnt fish and cabbage assaulted his nose.

"And if we disagree?" John asked.

"Then I dissolve our partnership. You cannot survive in this business without my expertise and supply of high-quality material." Haring stood. "I'll wait two days for your response. Have a nice evening, gentlemen."

John watched Haring leave, then used the ships internal communication system to dial a number. "Eddy, I have a job for you. Want it clean and untraceable."

After John disconnected, Brian said, "What are you doing? We need the Commodore's drugs."

"I'm terminating the relationship. I've been nervous since those two Smithsonian agents showed up. They have proven my fears to be right. But we need to address the problem, not put our tails between our legs and run. I managed to acquire another source to supply us, and at a better rate. We also need to address the future expectancy of those two women."

Brian's expression hardened. "You should have talked to me first. We are a partnership." He rose and stormed out of the galley.

"Another weak link to watch," mumbled John.

CHAPTER 32

Early the next morning, Virginia sat on an upholstered chair in the living room, sipping her coffee and enjoying the sunrise over the now calm Gulf of Mexico.

James Thornwood entered and took the chair near the eighty-inch television. "Good morning, Virginia. Where is Terry?"

"She's working up in the safe room with the relics."

James nodded. "I see." Using a remote control, he turned on the TV. "Have you seen the morning news?"

Virginia shook her head. "No. Why?"

"Remember Commodore Richard Haring?"

"Sure. He's the head honcho at the yacht club. What about him, did he get promoted to rear admiral?"

"No. Some joggers down by the harbor found his body in the water early this morning. He's dead," James said.

"What! He's dead? Was it natural causes?"

"No, two small caliber bullets to the back of his head."

"That'll do it." Virginia set her cup on the side table. "Any clues as to the killers?"

"The police said they are following multiple avenues of the investigation."

Virginia chuckled. "In other words, they haven't got a clue."

"You could be right."

"Why would someone want to kill the Commodore?" Virginia asked.

James shrugged his shoulders. "I don't know. He seemed like a nice fellow."

"Besides being the big shot at the yacht club and having a big boat, what did he do for a living?"

James rubbed his forehead. "I think he owned and ran a travel agency, owned a local marine repair and supply company, and had some building rentals... small business centers and houses."

"He had a huge yacht and was a member of the yacht club. How could he afford that running a travel company, a boat repair shop, and owning some rental property?"

"I have no idea. He seemed to always have a lot of money. I never put much thought into it. Had breakfast yet?"

"Yes. Terry and I were up early. The storm was intense last night."

"You're right. But this place can take a Category 5 hurricane or an EF5 tornado." James pointed at the TV. "Here is the part of the news about Haring's murder."

Virginia watched the news segment about the murder of the Commodore. The reporter said the body was found by a jogger in the old warehouse area on the old wharf. The police were giving "no comment" as answers to their questions. The cameraman with the on-site reporter scanned the area where the body was found. In the background was the *Unicorn*. Virginia stood. "I need to tell Terry about this. Thanks for bringing it to my attention." She hurried out of the room.

Entering the safe room with the relics, she found Terry, dressed in a red polo shirt and black jeans, covered in cobwebs, dancing around to the music on a radio. Terry jerked to a stop and smiled.

Virginia frowned. "What are you doing? Why are you covered with dirt?"

"I've been exploring."

"I figured that."

"I found the green dragon statue," Terry said proudly.

Virginia's eyes flickered with surprise. "You did? Where?"

"Like you, or Andy said, it was in plain sight. I used the secret tunnels and went to the library right after we had breakfast." Terry cleared her throat. "As you are aware, the room looks like something out of a movie set in an old English manor. There are walnut paneled walls, a wall length bookcase, huge stone fireplace, oversized leather chairs and sofas, and highly polished wooden tables."

"Yes, I've seen it."

"There are a lot of rare antiques on display in there, along with old books, various fossils, and memorabilia. So, I thought I'd start there. I looked around, and presto, on top of the bookshelf next to the fireplace was the green dragon statue. The other things up there were a little dusty, except for the dragon. It's obvious someone has been doing something with it recently."

"Where is it now?"

"I left it there." Terry pulled up a lab stool and sat. "I couldn't put it in our rooms, nor bring it here. So, I left it where it was."

"Good thinking. How big is it?"

"The size of a computer printer. It's heavy. I couldn't get it down from the shelf by myself."

"Nice work. I wonder what someone was doing with it. We need to take a closer look at it. Maybe we can use it to catch the antiquities trader and con artist. Like you said, we need hard evidence. But the reason I came up here looking for you is to tell you Commodore Haring has been murdered. They found his body this morning in the bay near the *Unicorn*.

"Why would someone kill him? He's a social fixture around town," Terry said.

"He was the head of the drug operation. It was his lab and drugs we destroyed, and Harry the Dragon belonged to him or his drug organization."

"Oh. I'm not surprised. How'd you figure that out?"

Virginia counted on her fingers. "Four reasons. He was a part owner of the *Unicorn* and was too knowledgeable about the men who operate it. He was upset when he heard about the lab and drugs being destroyed. He lives well above his reported means. And he knew a lot about Buckman Island."

"I see, I think. That seems a little shallow for evidence of his being a drug king, but he's dead, so that part of our investigation is finished," Terry said. "The local police can find his murderer."

"If Haring was murdered by his coconspirators, then we are in their sights as well. Looks like our taking Harry the Dragon was the last straw between them. Someone is restructuring their organization."

Terry watched Virginia, then closed her eyes, hung her head, and said, "You want to destroy the rest of the drug operation and find out who killed Haring. Don't forget, we've still got Sir Edward's murder to solve and a relics selling operation to stop."

Virginia gave her a mischievous grin. "Right on all counts."

"We're going to clandestinely go search the *Unicorn* for drugs tonight, aren't we?" Terry sighed. "Are you trying to get us killed?"

Virginia shook her head causing her blonde hair to get in her eyes. She wiped the hairs away and said, "No. Not tonight. I think our druggies will make a move on us, so we won't have to do any inspection of the *Unicorn*, at least not now. For the present, I want to take a look at the green stone dragon you found. That thing is important to someone, and we need to find out what it is. I believe it has to do with the death of Sir Edward."

"It'll take two of us to retrieve it, Terry said. "Do you want to bring it here to the lab?"

"We're going to have to. We can examine it better here."

"Then what do we do with it?" Terry asked.

"We'll cross that bridge when the time comes."

Terry pulled her cell phone from her pocket. "When I gave the green dragon statue a cursory examination, I took a couple of pictures. There is something unusual about the way it's carved and there is something... irregular about it." She scrolled through photographs on her phone, then stopped. She turned the phone around and showed the pictures to Virginia.

Dragon Threads

"See what I mean?"

Virginia studied the photographs, then with wide eyes, she looked at Terry. "Yes, I see it. We need that dragon now. Let's get our guns and fetch the little green guy."

"Okay, we snag the green dragon, we examine it, then what?"

"We hide it. Someone will take issue with the dragon turning up missing and come look for it. We may have both the drug people and the antiquities folks looking for us at the same time. Who knows, maybe it's the same gang. Then we have the hard evidence we need."

"Great. Two sets of killers after us." Terry sneezed. "Damn dust. Okay, let's get our weapons and meet in your room. I'm dying to examine that green dragon."

Virginia's face grew pensive. "Under these conditions, those aren't the words I would have chosen."

CHAPTER 33

Virginia changed into jeans and a chambray-colored shirt, attached her holster, and inserted a stainless-steel, .38 special revolver. Then she slipped a penlight into her pocket. After rummaging through her closet and locating her tan, L.L. Bean canvas carryall, she held it up and appraised it. *If the green stone dragon is the size of a computer printer, then this may work to carry it.* Virginia carried the bag into the parlor of her suite when Terry opened the door and strolled in.

Terry, with a semiautomatic in a holster on her right hip, eyed the bag. "Going shopping?"

"Yes, for a green dragon statue." She held up the carryall. "Is this big enough to fit your dragon statue?"

"Yep. That bag should do it."

Virginia set the bag down on a side table. "I think we should use the secret tunnels. No reason to go skulking down the halls armed and being observed."

Terry nodded. "Agreed. That's how I did it when I found the little guy."

Virginia picked up her bag and led Terry into her bedroom closet, turned the ceramic hook, and opened the back wall. They entered the dark, musty tunnel. Virginia and Terry switched on their lights and proceeded to the ladder. They quietly climbed down four floors to the first floor. Then they made their way to the hidden entrance to the library.

Terry opened the small peephole and looked into the room. "I don't see anyone. Let's go." She released the locking lever and pushed the bookcase open.

Virginia quickly followed Terry across the tartan plaid carpet, sitting atop the polished hardwood floor, to the bookcase next to the fireplace. Terry pointed. "There it is."

Virginia looked up at the green dragon, tucked close to the chimney. "How did you get up there?"

"I'll show you." Terry walked to the far side of the room and pushed a tall, polished, wooden stepladder across the room. "This is just the right height for us."

Virginia examined the stepladder. "If you say so."

Terry set the stepladder in front of the bookcase and climbed up. "Hand me the bag."

Virginia hoisted up the canvas bag. "Do you need help?"

"I can get it into the bag, but then I'll need to hand it down to you. I can't carry it and get down."

"Okay. Go for it." Virginia hurried to the closed main entrance doors and listened for any footfalls. She turned and rushed back when Terry called her. Reaching up, Virginia carefully took the bag and almost dropped it because of the sudden weight when Terry released her grip on the handle. "You're right, this is heavy."

Terry scampered down the stepladder and returned it to its original location, then darted back to Virginia. "Let's get this to the lab before anyone misses it."

Virginia, lugging the heavy carryall, led the way to the opening to the secret tunnels and entered. Terry closed the panel behind them. They slowly made their way up to the fourth floor and the antiquities lab, opened the secret panel, and entered. Virginia set the carryall on a lab bench and plopped onto a stool. "That dragon gained weight as we climbed up here."

"I don't doubt it," Terry said. "I could have helped you."

"You could have, but I wanted you fresh to examine this thing." Virginia opened the carryall and grunted as she pulled the green dragon out and set it on the table. "Okay, Dr. Sorenson, do your thing."

Terry went to another table and returned with a few inspection and measuring tools. She sat on a lab stool and slowly turned the dragon around, visually examining the object. "Look here," she pointed to three spots on the surface. "The way this is carved at these places is different than the rest of the surface."

Virginia bent over and looked. "I see what you mean. When you showed me the pictures, it seemed that there were a couple of other irregularities."

Terry rotated the dragon and inspected the neck. "You mean here?"

Virginia squinted. "Yes, what is that?"

"Since this thing is hundreds of years old, I mean the dragon was made from the meteorite hundreds of years ago, I think we can rule out a hologram."

"We need to figure out what that is."

Terry moved a magnifier in front of her and lowered the optics. She peered through it. "There is something here, but we need more power. I'll be right back." She hopped off the stool and went to a large, white moveable unit in the far corner of the laboratory. She pushed it to the table and plugged it into the electrical receptacle on the back of the table the dragon was on. "Give me a hand."

Virginia and Terry manhandled the stone dragon onto the portable device. Terry adjusted the position and turned on the machine. They looked at the viewing screen as Terry adjusted the focus. "Okay now we are getting a better view."

Virginia stared at the screen. "That looks like Old English or some type of language I can't read."

"You are correct. It's a mix of Old English and French," Terry said.

"Why would someone write it like that? And it is very tiny. That took some craftsmanship."

"Whoever wrote it didn't want just anyone to be able to read it. Not everyone was literate back in the 1100s, especially with two languages. Like today, Old English would be like a foreign one to most Englishmen back then. It's like a code. And it wasn't put here hundreds of years ago."

"When was it added? Any idea?"

"Recently, by the looks of it," Terry replied.

"Any idea what it says?"

Terry sat back. "Yes."

Virginia gave Terry an exasperated look. "Well?"

"You need some background first." Terry leaned on the table. "Henry II was King of England from 1154 until his death in 1189. And as such, Henry II was the first Angevin king of England."

Virginia pulled up another lab stool and sat. "I vaguely remember something about that from a class I took."

"Probably. Now, King Louis VII of France made him Duke of Normandy in 1150. Henry became Count of Anjou and Maine upon the death of his father, Count Geoffrey V, in 1151. His marriage in 1152 to Eleanor of Aquitaine, former spouse of Louis VII, made him Duke of Aquitaine. He became the Count of Nantes by treaty in 1158. Before he was 40, he controlled England, large parts of Wales, the eastern half of Ireland, and the western half of France. At various times, Henry also partially controlled Scotland and the Duchy of Brittany. It was the efforts of his mother, Matilda, daughter of Henry I of England, to claim the English throne, then occupied by Stephen Blois. Stephen agreed to a peace treaty after Henry's military expedition to England in 1153, and Henry inherited the kingdom on Stephen's death a year later."

Virginia shook her head. "You've done your homework."

"When we figured out when and where the meteor struck and knew it was during King Henry's reign, I looked him up."

"Okay, I've now got more information about King Henry II than I ever thought I'd need. So, what's with the hard-to-find Old English and French inscription? What did you mean it isn't hundreds of years old?"

Dragon Threads

Terry started to speak when she abruptly stopped and listened. "Someone is coming, we need to hide this green guy."

Virginia jumped to her feet. "You hide it, and I'll intercept whoever is approaching the lab."

CHAPTER 34

In the relics lab on the fourth floor, Virginia raced around the lab tables and equipment to the steel door and whipped the handle on the side of the door down, engaging the deadbolts. She took a breath and peered through the peephole. "Oh boy. This isn't good." She glanced over her shoulder, noting Terry near the rear wall cabinet. "We've got trouble. Did you hide the dragon?"

Terry nodded. "Yes. I also rearranged this shelving to look like we hastily did something here so no one will notice the dragon. Create a diversion, I hope."

"Can you lock the secret door to the tunnels?"

"I don't know. I'll check. Who's outside the main door?"

"The captain and owner of the *Unicorn,* John McDougal, the second officer Brian Kinman, a couple of henchmen, and James Thornwood."

"You suspected James for a while, haven't you?" Terry asked.

Virginia looked through the peephole again. "Yes. I figured him for the antiquities fraud, but not the drugs."

"Maybe he doesn't have anything to do with the drugs."

"Then why is he here with the *Unicorn's* people?" Virginia asked.

"They could be involved with both and not James."

Virginia shrugged her shoulder. "I guess that's possible. But they are now at the door and trying to open it."

"Can they get past the deadbolts?"

"Probably not, but we're basically stuck in here. Can you lock the entrance to the secret passages?"

Terry turned from the hidden doorway. "No. If they come this way, we may have to shoot it out."

"Try your cell phone and call Detective Moon."

"This place is basically a grounded, steel vault. No electronic signals can get in or out."

Virginia jumped at the pounding on the steel door. Her pulse felt elevated, and she was breathing hard. "Let's grab the dragon and get out of

Dodge. If they are outside this door, then they aren't in the tunnels."

"You hope."

"If we can get downstairs, we may be able to get out of the house or into the underground tunnels and the exits before they mount another assault through the passageway."

Terry rubbed her palms on her pantlegs and swallowed. "I'll get the dragon."

Virginia looked through the peephole again. "James is still here looking at his cell phone. The others are heading away."

Terry stood holding the canvas carryall. "Got the dragon. If we're going to use the passageways, then we'd better hurry. I bet the guys from the ship are going to find an entrance to the secret passages and try to storm their way in here."

Virginia rushed to Terry. She grabbed a large cardboard box, placed five fake relics in it, ran strapping tape across the top to seal it, and then, carrying the box, Virginia led them out of the laboratory into the secret passageway.

They hurried down the tunnel to the first ladder. Terry climbed down with the carryall containing the dragon. Virginia hesitated. "I can't climb down with this box. It's too clumsy and heavy."

"If you drop it down here maybe I can catch it."

"It weighs too much," Virginia said. "I'll leave it here. If they come this way, maybe in the time it will take to open it and discover it hasn't got the dragon in it, we can get away."

"Okay. Hurry."

Virginia set the box against the back wall of the tunnel and partially covered it with a few loose boards that were laying on the floor. She then hastened down the ladder. "Okay, decoy set. Let's get out of here fast."

They continued down the ladders to the first floor. They quickly moved through the passages until they arrived at the entrance to the kitchen. They moved the cover of the peephole and looked into the kitchen through the doorway in the butler's pantry. Emma, the kitchen helper, was standing at the island mixing something in a large glass bowel. Jason was at the stove with his back towards Virginia. Virginia turned to Terry. "Emma and Jason are in there."

"Want to find another way out?"

"This is the fastest way, so if we…"

"Waltz in and nonchalantly amble through the kitchen, they won't notice?"

"Something like that." Virginia pulled her pistol, smiled, and said, "Just a little insurance."

Terry nodded then turned the handle and opened the hidden entrance to the kitchen. She pushed the shelf open, carefully entered the butler's pantry, and looked around. Seeing no one, she ventured into the pantry. Virginia entered behind her and took the lead. They walked into the kitchen. Jason and Emma turned and looked at them, then spotted Virginia's gun. Emma gasped.

Virginia put her finger to her lips. "Please don't yell. We are not going to hurt anyone. We need to get out without..."

"The others seeing you?" Jason asked.

"That's it in a nutshell."

Emma nodded, then Jason tossed Virginia two keys. "The red key is for the red cabin cruiser. It's fast. The black one is for the ATV outside the door. Go. We can delay them a little if they come this way."

Terry tilted her head. "Why are you doing this?"

"You have the green dragon in that bag, don't you?" asked Emma.

Terry nodded. "You know about it?"

"Yes. I was recently approached by another museum who spent years researching it, and they wanted me to locate that dragon for them," Emma stated. "Jason has been helping me."

Virginia's eyes widened. "Another museum? Then why help us?"

"Hey, I'm just a freelance relic hunter in my spare time," Emma said. "I don't have the resources you have, and I don't want those crooks to get it. The museum wants the dragon, but it's better if you protect it. This isn't a turf war, after all. I know there's something about it that people want. Maybe directions to a treasure... who knows?"

Virginia looked at Jason. "And how did you get involved in relic hunting?"

"Emma asked for my help, and in return, she promised to help me find the people responsible for what happened to my sister. Since it looks like the people looking for the dragon might be responsible for both, I agreed.

"Now go while you have the advantage," Emma hissed. "I don't want bullets or blood on my floors."

"Okay. Thanks." Virginia stepped to the rear door and glanced outside. The black ATV was parked ten feet away. Seeing no one, she and Terry bolted for the vehicle.

CHAPTER 35

Terry jumped into the ATV's passenger seat as Virginia climbed in behind the steering wheel. She started the motor and sped off toward the boathouse. As she wound down the asphalt path, Terry asked, "Jason said to take the cabin cruiser. Why not get our car and just drive off the island?"

"They have armed guards at the checkpoint where the driveway meets the public road. It's probably blocked."

Terry nodded. "Right. The boat it is."

Virginia steered toward the boathouse. A couple minutes later, she brought the ATV to a sliding stop. "Let's find that cabin cruiser."

They jumped out of the ATV and entered the boat shed. At the end of the inside pier sat the red cabin cruiser Jason mentioned. They hurried to the boat. Virginia hopped onto the rear deck and took the carryall with the dragon statue, while Terry untied the lines.

Virginia tried to start the boat. The engine coughed, then fell silent. She tried again, and this time the engine sputtered to life. Virginia backed away from the slip and turned toward the Gulf of Mexico. She pushed the throttles to the stops, and the boat shot out of the shed, sending back a wide wake as the boat sliced through the water. "Terry, use your cell phone and call Commander Linman at the Coast Guard station. Get us some help."

Terry, staring back at the manor, frowned. "Why? We got away."

Virginia pointed. "The *Unicorn* is coming at us from the north. That's a big boat, and they can handle the waves better than we can. They probably have armed men ready to shoot us if we don't stop. We may be able to outrun them or get into shallow water, but they have guns, probably rifles."

"Calling the Coast Guard."

The cabin cruiser slammed hard against the small swells as it sped down the coast. After a ten-minute pounding ride, Virginia noticed the *Unicorn* was gaining on them. Then the radio squawked. "This is the *Unicorn;* stop your motor, give us the dragon, and we won't hurt you."

Cold fingers brushed Virginia's heart. She picked up the microphone and pressed the talk button. "We will not comply with your demand." She and Terry ducked as rifle bullets struck the boat. Virginia pressed the talk button again. "That was not very neighborly."

"Stop, or we will take the dragon by force and sink you."

Virginia kept the throttles wide open and swung the boat left and right, making them a harder target to shoot. More bullets struck the stern, and a few shots hit the cabin.

Terry pulled her pistol out and, staying low, started for the stern. Virginia grabbed her shoulder. "That wouldn't do much good. They are out of effective pistol range."

Terry slid her gun back into its holster. "Any other ideas? That damn *Unicorn* is gaining on us."

"Did you get through to Commander Linman?"

"No. I talked to a lieutenant. He said he would forward our message to the Commander."

"Great. Just great. I think we're going to have to come up with our own plan B."

Terry sighed. Then, looking out into the Gulf of Mexico, she straightened. "Look over there."

Virginia turned and squinted. "That's a Coast Guard ship, and she's coming this way fast. Maybe they'll get here before we're fish food." She tilted her head and listened as the thump-thump of helicopter rotors roared over their heads.

She told Terry to take the helm, rushed to the back of the cabin, and looked up. A large gray U.S. Navy helicopter, with its side door open and a man in a sling manning a 50-caliber machine gun, flew over in the direction of the *Unicorn* and circled it. She watched and listened as someone spoke over the chopper's loudspeaker. "Stop your engines and stand-by for boarding by the U.S. Coast Guard. Failure to comply will result in our opening fire and sinking your vessel."

The *Unicorn* continued to steam ahead. The chopper shot across the bow with its 50-caliber machine gun. The *Unicorn* stopped and rode the swells as the navy helicopter orbited.

The cabin cruiser's radio squawked again. "This is Lieutenant Alcott, U.S. Coast Guard. Virginia Davies Clark in the red cabin cruiser, please proceed to the Coast Guard station on Galveston Island."

Virginia rushed forward, took the mic from Terry, and responded. "This is Virginia. Changing heading for Coast Guard station. Where are you?"

"I'm on the cutter to your south with Coast Guard Investigative Service Agents rapidly approaching your location. We have orders to handle the *Unicorn.*"

"If I may ask, what's with the Navy chopper?" Virginia turned on the windshield wiper as sea spray splattered the glass.

Dragon Threads

"We were too far away to quickly assist you, so we enlisted help from the Navy."

"Good. Thank you."

"One more thing, Detective Moon is raiding the manor as we speak."

Virginia gave a sigh of relief. "We'll call him to tell him who the bad guys are."

"No need. He'll just bring everyone to the police station, and you can sort things out there."

"Lieutenant, there are over six hundred pounds of meth and fentanyl on the *Unicorn* in some sort of hidden hold. And I think Commodore Richard Haring of the Lost Harbor Yacht Club was murdered on that ship."

"Thanks for the tips. We'll handle it from here. Coast Guard out."

Virginia turned to Terry, who was watching the helicopter. "After we go to the Coast Guard station, they'll probably take us to the police station to sort everything out." Virginia stared ahead as she steered the boat, then said, "Call Detective Moon and tell him how to get into the secret passages and underground tunnels. He needs to see the workshop where they copy artifacts."

"Okay." Terry called the detective. After disconnecting, she said, "Would you like to know what the tiny inscription on the green dragon says?"

Virginia nodded. "Sure, but now?"

"This is as good a time as any."

Virginia ran her hands around the wooden steering wheel. "Okay, what does it say?"

"It tells where King Richard II's secret treasure is hidden."

"The what?" Virginia asked with a puzzled expression.

"Somewhere around 1000 AD, during a castle uprising, Richard II had to flee with... some say treasure... but more likely money and valuables he obtained from Lords and other people in some shady deals. To hide it, he gave it to Lord Buckman for safe keeping until the uprising could be put down, or so the story goes."

"How'd the King or Buckman lose it? Playing poker?"

Terry chuckled. "Cute. No, Buckman hid it, and then history gets murky. After things calmed down at the royal court, the King wanted his treasure back. But Lord Buckman died suddenly, and the treasure was lost."

"But our green dragon friend knows where it is?"

"So it seems," said Terry. "The location of the treasure was lost. But a story about it lingered as a Buckman oral history, handed down verbally to each new Buckman lord. Finally, it was detailed on the green dragon. Remember, it was the only thing on top of that bookcase that didn't have dust on it. I think Sir Edward did it just before he was murdered."

"Wait a minute." Virginia turned the boat slightly starboard to pass a slower boat. "You're right. The green dragon's tiny inscription appeared to be done by a laser. They didn't have lasers in the 1100s."

Terry nodded. "The letters are miniscule, and the sharpness makes me think you are correct. Hence, Sir Edward."

"So, then one of the Buckman lords found the treasure and moved it to Texas?"

"That's what this suggests. I think the Buckman who moved it here was one of Sir Edward's predecessors."

"Why move it here?"

"Maybe because the British Crown owns it, and the Buckman's would probably not get anything, or just a small reward for finding it in England. Here in Texas, it's his. If he doesn't make a big deal of it, and sells some of the treasure slowly and widely; then neither the Crown nor our IRS will get wind of the treasure. He's the main benefactor."

"He put directions to the location of the treasure on the dragon. I think you're right, maybe it was Sir Edward."

Terry grabbed the armrest of her seat as the boat rolled slightly. "There is a laser in the workroom where the artifacts are stored."

"So, someone else knew he hid the treasure. But why kill him?"

"Good question. Maybe to stop him from giving away the secret of the directions to the treasure. Or... maybe they wanted it for themselves and killed him before he could divulge the treasure's location."

Virginia eyed Terry who was grinning. "You already know where the treasure is, don't you?"

Terry gave a conspiratorial smile. "I bet it's hidden at the manor."

Virginia arched a speculative eyebrow. "In the manor? Where in the manor?"

"I don't know. We need both our green dragon friend and the quilt to figure that part out."

"Why do we need the quilt?"

"Because, according to the inscription on the dragon, the second part of the instructions are on the quilt," Terry answered. "Needing both the quilt and the dragon to locate the treasure was an added layer of security. Who knew that someone would wrap a bunch of bones in that quilt? By the way, you left the quilt at the manor."

Virginia shook her head. "Great. After we're done with the Coast Guard and Detective Moon, we need to get back to the manor and retrieve the quilt before someone else snags it."

"Let's hope the cops don't have it."

Virginia changed direction again to head the boat into the waves. "How would Buckman get a treasure into the U.S. undetected?"

"Besides being landed gentry in England, the Buckman's were relic hunters and smugglers. And, as estate owners, baronets, and lords, they have connections in the right circles in both the U.S. and England. And they probably needed the extra money to pay the exorbitant British taxes on their estate and income."

The radio squawked again. Annoyed by the interruption, Virginia picked up the mic and said in a curt voice, "This is Virginia."

"Virginia, this is Detective Moon."

Her voice softened. "Hi, how'd the raid go?"

"Based on your and Dr. Sorenson's notes, and what we found there, we arrested everyone at the manor except the kitchen staff... Jason and Emma. I have men going through the tunnels now. So far, we've got enough from what we found here, along with what the Coast Guard found on the *Unicorn,* to put these people away for a long time."

"Great."

"I was instructed by the Smithsonian to leave the relics and artifacts and the selling of fakes to you."

"Good. We'll get to work on that as soon as we get back. Do you want us to come to the police station or will you meet us at the Coast Guard facility?"

"Neither right now. You've got work to do. We can talk later. But... I've got some bad news. James Thornwood got away."

CHAPTER 36

Virginia nosed the cabin cruiser into its slip at the boathouse. Terry hopped off and tied the lines to hold the boat firmly in place. They took the carryall with the green dragon statue and hurried to the ATV. Virginia gunned the engine. As the ATV sped toward the manor, Terry glanced toward the Gulf. "Looks like that storm is growing and getting closer. I thought the Texas beaches were for sun and fun."

Virginia chuckled. "I think the state will have to sue Mother Nature or pass a no rain or storm along the coast law. After all, Palm Springs, California, has a city ordinance against rain. It seems to work out for them."

"Very funny. Once we get to the manor, then what?"

"We grab the quilt, use it and the dragon to locate the treasure, and hope no one interferes."

"Okay, but how do we handle the relic forgeries and trafficking in antiquities? Everyone is in police custody."

Virginia slowed as the ATV approached the manor's kitchen entrance. "Once we have the treasure, I'll bet the perpetrators will come to us."

"Great. We get to be bait again," mumbled Terry. "At least this time I don't have to wear my new, red, dental floss bikini."

"You were very popular with the men wearing it." Virginia parked the ATV and slid out. Terry climbed out, holding the carryall with the dragon, and followed Virginia into the kitchen.

Terry looked around the empty room. "Where are Jason and Emma?"

"I don't know. The police left them behind, so they are around here somewhere or decided to leave the island on their own."

"Since the place is empty, maybe they're looking for the treasure. The people responsible for Jason's sister should be in custody by now."

"You could be right. Emma did say she's a relic hunter, and Jason is helping her. Now, let's get the quilt."

Terry leaned close and whispered. "We'd better be quiet. No telling who's where. And you left the dragon quilt in a blue pillowcase in the antiquities lab."

Virginia shook her head. "No. That pillowcase is a ruse."

"It is? Then where is it?"

"The quilt is in my room. It's behind the TV."

Terry froze. "Behind the TV? Then the cops have it."

"Why?"

"It wouldn't be that hard to find."

"The police weren't looking for a quilt. And I don't think they searched our rooms. Remember, we're feds."

"Then let's go get it and figure this puzzle out." Terry turned and looked at the kitchen window. "I thought I heard something. It's raining again. I think I'll sue Mother Nature."

Virginia led the way up to the fourth floor and her rooms. She hurried to the built-in shelving and the TV sitting in the central part, reached behind it, and pulled out the rolled-up dragon quilt. "Better lock the door. Now we can see what the dragon statue and the quilt have to say."

Terry set the carryall down. "I think we should use the lab. It's got the high-power magnifiers, which will make it easier to read what's inscribed on the dragon, and it would probably be safer."

Virginia pursed her lips and nodded. "Good idea."

They hurried to the lab. The steel doors were still locked from the inside. Virginia sighed. "We locked them when we were here before and left through the tunnels. I guess we go back the same way."

Virginia carried the quilt, while Terry lugged the carryall with the dragon back to Virginia's room. They hurried to her closet and stepped into the tunnel. Using her Maglite, Virginia illuminated their way to the lab. They opened the passageway door to the well-lit laboratory.

Virginia turned off the flashlight and stepped inside. She moved to the workbench where the magnifier sat. She placed the quilt on the counter as Terry moved beside her, set the carryall on the tabletop, withdrew the dragon, and placed it next to the magnifier.

Terry started to speak when Virginia suddenly put her finger to her lips. She whispered, "Quiet. There is something or someone behind that spectrograph machine." Virginia pulled her revolver and quietly padded toward the machine. Terry, gun drawn, followed a few feet behind and to the right of Virginia. They stopped. Virginia spoke with a sharp tone, "You, hiding behind this machine. Raise your hands and step out where we can see you. If you have anything in your hands you can't eat, we will shoot you."

Muffled sounds came from behind the machine. Terry cautiously moved closer and looked behind the spectrograph over the top of her pistol. She sighed and lowered her weapon. "Virginia, you'd better see this."

Virginia edged her way forward and peered over the machine. She lowered her weapon and ran her hand across the back of her neck. "Okay, let's get them out of there."

Terry pulled a pocketknife from her pocket, cut the plastic ties from the wrists and ankles of Jason and Emma, and removed their gags.

Jason and Emma rose rubbing their wrists. Jason cleared his throat. "Thank you. We thought—"

Emma completed his sentence, "When you came in, we thought you were the relic thieves coming back."

"How long have you been in here?" Terry asked.

"From right after you took off with the ATV. The men who tried to get into this room when you were here came storming into the kitchen after you left. They grabbed us. Some of them were from the *Unicorn.*"

Virginia frowned. "The main door is still locked from the inside. How'd you get in here?"

Jason swallowed. "One of the men knew about the passageways. They brought us here the same way you got in and out."

"Let me guess, their leader was James Thornwood IV."

Emma looked at her shoes. "Yes. I never suspected him. I thought he was a nice man."

"Well, you're safe with us now," Terry said. "Do you know where James is at the moment?"

"We heard the police in the building and thought they might have taken him with them when they left. We were hoping the police would get the steel door open, but they didn't. They had no idea that the secret passageways existed. I'm sure they were not aware of the tunnels on the island either."

Virginia nodded. "The police know about the tunnels. I told them. But I'm surprised they didn't locate these passages and you." She took a side glance at the green dragon, then said, "Why don't you and Jason go downstairs and have a cup of tea in the dining room to relax and recover while Terry and I take stock of things?"

Jason reached for Emma's hand. "I think Virginia has a good idea. Let's go." He stopped and turned to Virginia. "Would you like me to make some for you two as well?"

Virginia smiled. "Maybe later."

Terry watched Jason unbolt and open the steel door and leave with Emma. She turned to Virginia. "What was that all about?"

"Lock the door. The game's afoot—let's decipher the dragon and the quilt, locate the treasure, and prepare for trouble. It'll come on strong shortly."

CHAPTER 37

Virginia set the dragon statue on the workbench and unfolded the dragon quilt. She watched Terry move the high-power microscope next to the bench and attach the large viewscreen.

Terry nodded. "All set. Let's put our dragon on this surface first and position it." With Virginia's help, Terry moved the dragon and set it in a rotation jig and sat on a lab stool. "Okay. Let's see what we've got." Terry flipped a couple toggle switches, turned a knob, then pushed a yellow button. The image of part of the dragon appeared on the screen. She rotated the statue until the laser marking appeared. "I can read the French sections. It says, Henry II's bounty was moved from England to a site here in south Texas. The whole treasure is now back together for the first time. I can't decipher this part, but it says something about a dungeon." Terry leaned back. "Old English isn't in my wheelhouse I'm afraid." She jumped as a loud clap of thunder sounded.

"The storm is getting worse." Virginia moved Terry off the stool and sat. She pointed at the control panel. "This knob enlarges the image?"

"Yes."

"My Old English is very rusty. My forte is American history. But since there isn't an Old English scholar handy, I'll do my best." Virginia squinted at the screen. "Good thing Sir Edward used the laser to write this, it's extremely tiny. This part isn't much help. It tells where the treasure was hidden in England." Virginia laughed. "It was taken to France and hidden in The Royal Abbey of Our Lady of Fontevraud. Makes sense." She looked away from the screen and at Terry. "Henry was big in France. The King of England, Henry II, his wife, Eleanor of Aquitaine, and their son, King Richard the Lionheart, were all buried here at the end of the 12th century. It was seized and disestablished as a monastery during the French Revolution. No one found the hidden treasure for all those years. But according to this, it finally had to be moved. The Abbey was taken over a few more times and was last a prison. Now it is owned by the French Ministry of Culture." Virginia looked up as the overhead light fixture flickered. "That's not good.

The storm must be getting worse."

Terry leaned closer to the monitor. "Your Old English is rusty? You're on a roll, girl. What else does it say?"

"Sir Edward's great grandfather retrieved the treasure and hid it at an old pub he owned near Stratford-upon-Avon. Sir Edward is the one who moved it to the United States and finally to Texas."

"Anything about the dungeon?"

"No. But it does say a certain wall-hanging sized green dragon quilt holds the clue."

Terry picked up the quilt from the workbench. "So, the location of the dungeon and the treasure are on this somewhere?"

"That's what it says." The overhead lights flickered. The room reverberated from the sound of booming thunder nearby. "That's not good. This joint has a backup generator, doesn't it?" Virginia looked at Terry. She was frozen stiff. "What's wrong?"

A male voice behind her answered. "Yes, Virginia, this joint has a generator."

Virginia felt her heart start to pound in her chest. She slowly turned around. Seeing James holding a semiautomatic on them, her resolve set harder than granite counters. "Hello James. I wondered when you would show up."

"You knew?"

"Of course, I knew. Back when I arrived, someone took a shot at you, or us. The window is bullet and storm proof. It didn't faze you as much as it should have. Then we heard some of the men who were working in the tunnels with the drugs say James wanted it moved that night. And you were with the men from the *Unicorn* who tried to storm this lab. I didn't understand why you didn't tell them about the secret tunnels."

He nodded. "I didn't tell them because I didn't want to share the treasure with them."

"You were in league with Commodore Haring and the drug operation?"

"Yes. We had a deal. I provided the space for their lab and a means of smuggling the drugs out, and the use of Harry the dragon to ensure nosy neighbors and boaters didn't interfere, for a percentage of the gross proceeds." James waved his arm. "Upkeep for all this costs a lot of money."

"How about the relics and antiquities?"

"Now that was mine. Quite lucrative. I wasn't sharing that with those crazed druggies. I was doing quite well until Sir Edward arrived. I had no idea he was here yet, and when I learned why he came and that he discovered my drug and antiquities ventures, well, something had to be done. The royal treasure will go a long way to preserve the lifestyle I deserve."

Virginia shrugged her shoulder. "I get that. So, what now?"

Dragon Threads

James sneered at her. "You and Dr. Terry are going to take me to the treasure."

Virginia stared at him.

"Now!" He waved the pistol. "I haven't got a lot of time."

Virginia wet her lips. "I think we should negotiate some sort of agreement first, a finder's fee if you will."

He lowered his weapon slightly and chuckled. "In case it escaped your notice, I have the gun. So here is the deal. I get all the treasure and you two may live."

Virginia frowned. "May live? That's not acceptable."

"How about this? You show me the treasure and I won't kill Dr. Terry."

The room shook from another clap of thunder, then the lights went out. A couple of seconds later the lights came back on. James swung the gun around as he frantically looked around the lab. He was alone. *Where did they go so fast?* "Okay Virginia. You and Terry show yourselves or I will destroy the quilt." He stepped to the workbench and stared. "Shit! Where the hell is the quilt?" In its place was a playing card. The black Ace of Spades with his name on it and a bullet hole in it. He thought of what Virginia and Terry had done and the number of his men they had killed or injured while on the island. Fear rushed in a blood-pumping ripple through him. Time seemed to freeze to a crawl with the expectation that he might very well die, and soon. Attacking them was a huge mistake. He plopped onto the lab stool.

CHAPTER 38

Virginia and Terry scampered down the tunnel to the ladder. They quickly descended four floors to the ground level. They hurried via the passageway to the kitchen and peered through the peephole.

Virginia stepped back, leaned against the wall, and sighed. "There are armed men out there. Our only way to what might be a safe place is down through the tunnels under the island."

"We need a place to study the quilt," responded Terry. "We can't leave the treasure to this bunch of cutthroats."

"True. But we need to find such a place fast. I'm sure James knows this place better than anyone."

"Call Detective Moon," Terry said.

"Can't. I left my phone in the lab. Do you have yours?"

"Mine's in the lab, too."

Virginia's eyes widened. "I have an idea."

"This better be good."

"It'll get us off the island."

"It will?" Terry shook her head. "How? Just walk out there and tell the murderers in there we are taking our leave?"

"Something like that. We need to get to the boat shed."

"It might be guarded. And have you noticed the storm? The gulf won't be fit for man nor beast."

"It probably is guarded. And we aren't men nor beasts. But we have an advantage."

"We do?" Terry frowned. "What?"

Virginia held up the large cloth bag containing the Dragon quilt. "In here is the quilt. It also has my wallet, gun, badge case, and a Ketamine spray canister. I noticed you also grabbed the red bag when we hurried out of the lab. What's in yours?"

"Oh boy."

"Oh boy what?" Virginia asked. "We haven't much time. What's in your bag?"

"My gun, wallet, lab notebook, badge case, my new bright-red dental floss bikini, and a spray canister of SRH."

"I thought you might have that. Good. That's what we need."

"What?" Terry wrinkled her brow. "The spray or the bikini?"

"Both. You use the Shit Releasing Hormone spray on them. And we need to be up wind when we spray it. I remember the problem the people in the jungle had using it during our *Trail of Threads* investigation."

"Yeah, the wind turned, and it hit them instead of us. We can't have that happen here. There isn't much in the canister."

Virginia grabbed the door release lever. "Besides the spray, you can change into your new dental floss bikini and be the distraction again. Murderers they may be, but they are men. And trust me, Doctor, you are every man's dream in that bikini."

Terry grumbled. "Shit! I was hoping I wouldn't need to be another distraction."

"You'll do great. And wear that at a pool in Texas when we're out of here, and you'll have any male there eating out of your hand. Who knows, you might catch someone special with it."

"Let's get out of here, find the treasure, then plan my love life, such as it is."

"Okay. Get your gun and spray. I'll use the Ketamine spray." Virginia watched Terry get ready, then opened the door into the butler's pantry. They quickly exited the secret passageway. Virginia peeked around the corner and whispered. "There are four armed men. Fortunately, they have rifles."

"How's that lucky?"

"In a close environment like the kitchen, they are cumbersome to use. If we rush them, we have the element of surprise. Knock out and SRH sprays, and pistols."

"Where exactly are they?"

"Two by the stove, one at the rear door, and one by the entrance to the dining room door."

"They're in three locations. That's not good."

"I'll spray Ketamine at the two by the stove. You shoot the man by the dining room door and try for the guy blocking our escape. Then I'll use my pistol if necessary."

"Okay. Here goes nothing."

Virginia burst into the kitchen and sprayed the men by the stove before anyone noticed she and Terry were there. The men fell to the floor. Seconds behind Virginia, Terry shot the man by the dining room door, spreading blood across the doorway, and swung her weapon toward the guard by the rear door. She heard another gun fire and saw the man by the rear door, still trying to raise his rifle, fall face down on the floor after his head smashed into a counter. The floor was becoming slippery with blood. They hurried across the room and rushed outside into the rain, watching for any more adversaries. Seeing no one, they sprinted across the wet sand to the road toward the boat shed.

Now soaking wet, Terry ran next to Virginia. "When and where am I supposed to change into my distraction outfit? Is the quilt getting wet?"

"I forgot about that and no, the quilt is in a plastic bag."

"Good." Terry raised a brow. "Where'd you get the plastic?"

"It was already in the bag."

"Of course it was."

Virginia wiped a strand of wet blond hair from her face. "Now we'll just have to rush them."

"That's what General Custer said."

"He was a colonel at Big Horn. He was a temporary general during the Civil War."

"Really? Now?" Terry shook her head. "Just what I need right now, a U.S. history major."

"We'll be at the boat shed in a couple minutes," Virginia said. "When we get closer, we can hide behind a sand dune and reconnoiter."

"I hope the SRH stuff works in this rain." Lightening flashed and a clap of thunder followed in a few seconds. Terry shuddered. "That strike was close. We're lightning rods out here. Not good. I want to live long enough to at least try and get off the island."

"Not to worry. They are not expecting us." As they rounded a curve and tried to head into the dunes, a shot rang out, and a bullet whizzed by their heads from the direction of the boat shed.

Terry glanced at Virginia as they dove onto the wet sand and crawled out of the line of fire. "Not expecting us, General Custer?"

CHAPTER 39

Virginia peered over the top of a wet sand hill at the boat shed and the two men guarding it. She heard someone slosh through a puddle to her left. She slid down the sand and whispered to Terry. "Two men by the boat shed and one creeping up on us just around the edge of this dune."

Terry nodded. "I take out the one around the corner." She held up the spray can of SRH. "He'll make a lot of noise and smell like… well maybe the rain will help clean him up."

"Be careful. The ground is wet and slippery, and he knows we are here."

"I'll be careful. What are you going to do?"

"Take out the other two guards. Meet me in the boat shed."

"Got it. Be careful." Terry slid down the dune and disappeared from Virginia's sight.

Virginia heard some rustling in the scrub below as she maneuvered along the right side of the sand hill. *I wonder what Terry is going to do. Jump out and spray the guy? That would be risky.* She tugged at her wet shirt. *Crap. Now it's uncomfortable and see through. Of course, it's raining now. It's not just the wet shirt and shorts, it's the wet sand that gets everywhere.* She paused. *Wet shirt? Two men? I have an idea.* Virginia quickly removed her bra and closed her shirt. *Now I also have a distraction.*

She moved to the right side of the dune and, wiping rain from her face, slowly crept up on the boat shed. Glancing around a scrub bush, she noticed them looking in the direction the third man had taken. Virginia found a rock and tossed it toward the water near the two men. The thud of the rock landing in the wet sand caused them to turn and start for the area where they heard the noise. She rose. Her sudden appearance, wearing a see through shirt with nothing under it, surprised them. With their rifles pointed toward the ground, they stood and gawked.

Virginia aimed her gun at them. "Drop your weapons, or I will kill you."

The men continued to stare. She took a deep breath, "Drop your damn guns now!"

The taller man, wearing a yellow rain slicker and floppy hat, grinned and started to raise his gun. "You're too pretty to shoot anyone, girlie."

"Girlie?" Virginia shot him just as he raised his rifle level enough to aim at her. She moved to her left and aimed at the other man. He tossed his rifle away into the sand and lowered himself to the ground with his hands on his head just as they heard a cry from around the sand dune. It was the sound of the third man in serious pain. "That must be your partner who came looking for us."

Terry came around the dune carrying the man's rifle. "Looks like you have things under control." She stopped and frowned. "I see you used a distraction as well."

Virginia nodded. "Bare boobs will do that. Caught them off guard."

Terry pointed at the man face down in the sand. "Why'd you shoot him?"

"He called me girlie."

"Good thing he said it to you. You just shot and killed him. I would have shot off some appendages first."

The man on his knees cleared his throat. "I... I'm glad it was her now, too. What happened to Vern?"

Virginia bent down. "Who's Vern?"

"He went around the dune to see if you two were coming this way. Then you showed up. That sounded like him screaming a while ago." He pointed at Terry. "That's his rifle you're holding. Did you shoot him?"

Terry laughed. "No. I gave him a dose of a chemical. His bowels are releasing themselves in a painful, violent, and smelly manner right now."

The man frowned. "Huh?"

"He just shit his pants and will keep doing so for a while. He'll become severely dehydrated and extremely weak." Terry held up the spray canister. "Want to try some? Works fast."

His face twisted in fear. "No!"

Terry turned to Virginia. "I have some zip ties we can use on him, or you can shoot him."

The man looked down at his wet crotch. "Oh God."

Virginia chuckled. "Terry, you seem to have a way with men. Let's tie him up and stash him behind this dune. We've got work to do."

They used the plastic ties to bind the man and pulled him away from the shed and out of sight. Virginia led Terry into the boat shed. They walked along the wooden deck to the red cabin cruiser. Terry untied it and pushed the bow toward the opening to the gulf. Virginia climbed on board, started the engine, shifted her position, then pushed the throttles to their stops and jumped off the boat on to the deck, rolling to the far side as the boat shot out into the gulf.

Terry watched the boat charge into the angry water. "There goes our ride."

"We're not leaving... yet."

Terry walked toward the land entrance with Virginia. "We're not leaving? Did I miss something?"

"No. We're going back to the manor. James will think we left in the boat and either give chase or send some henchmen after us. He needs the quilt to locate the treasure."

"Okay. But why are we going back?"

"To arrest James and find the treasure," Virginia said.

"How do you know where the treasure is if you haven't had time to examine the quilt?" Terry asked.

"Because I think I understand the symbols I saw when I first examined it," Virginia replied. "I'll examine the quilt again to confirm I'm right after we take care of James."

"Shouldn't we should secure the treasure before we go after James?"

"If I'm right, it has been secure for a while, and James doesn't know where it is. We should get him first, then safely acquire the treasure."

"You have a point, but we'd better hide first. I think I got a glimpse of him storming this way."

Virginia led them around the boat shed to a pile of rocks, weeds, and driftwood. They watched as James, dressed in a yellow raincoat and a Dutch Harbor Sou'wester rain hat, stomped into the boathouse, then quickly returned outside. He raised a handheld radio to his lips and yelled over the roar of the surf and wind. "Get your forty-footer out and chase down the red cabin cruiser the women have taken. With the waves and wind, I'm sure they couldn't have gone far." He listened to the reply, then stated through clenched teeth, "I don't care about the storm, I want those two women brought back to me with the damn quilt. Now get on it."

Virginia frowned. "I wonder who he's talking to."

"I don't know."

He looked at the dead man. "They shot you. Vern is in deep shit and pain, but where is Ben?" He noted the rifle in the sand a couple feet from the surf line. "There's his rifle. They must have taken him."

Terry looked at Virginia. "He thinks we're on the cabin cruiser. His guard is down."

Virginia watched James. She looked at Terry and down at her wet, transparent blouse, then nodded. "Okay, we're already soaked to the skin. We can't get wetter, and you are right, he's not expecting us. Let's take him now."

CHAPTER 40

Virginia quietly rose and stepped out from the dune behind James. She aimed her gun at him, then yelled over the sounds of the wind and surf, "James Thornwood IV, you are under arrest. Put down any weapons and your radio, raise your hands, and get on your knees."

Thornwood slowly turned and stared at her. "You won't shoot me." He tilted his head, smiled, and said, "Like your shirt. Have you ever been in a wet t-shirt contest?"

"I just bet you do. And yes, I have been in a few wet t-shirt contests. Now, do as I said, or else."

"You can't shoot an unarmed man."

"I can't see what you have under your jacket, so as far as I'm concerned, you are armed until proven otherwise." Virginia noticed his finger repeatedly pushing a button on the radio. *He's signaling someone.*

James continued to smile. "I see the launching of the boat was a ruse. Good job. But now it's just you and me in this storm." He looked around. "Where is Dr. Sorenson?"

"Out in the boat. She's headed for Galveston."

"To summon help?"

"No. To get the treasure."

"Huh?"

"After Sir Edward found your antiquities fraud and drug operations, you didn't think he was dumb enough to leave it on this island?"

"I… well… no. I see what you mean. Maybe we can make a deal."

Virginia chuckled. "You're right. We can make a deal. You go to prison, and I get the treasure and return it to the English Crown."

"Virginia, let's be reasonable. You can't shoot me. I'm not armed, I'm bigger and stronger than you. I can take that gun of yours away from you and break your pretty neck."

"I'm not going to let you do that."

James shifted his stance. "I have a fourth-degree black belt in karate."

"I'm impressed. But I have a black belt in pistol, and my finger is already on the trigger. Want to test your karate skills against my bullet?" *He's stalling.*

"We could talk about my deal," James said.

"Which is?"

"We split the treasure sixty, forty."

"Who gets the sixty percent?"

"Me."

"I don't think so. I know where it is, and you don't. I get the sixty percent."

"Okay. You get sixty percent. Do we have a deal?"

Virginia noticed a grin on his face. *He's suddenly overconfident. Trouble.*

"Drop your gun, honey," stated a man from behind Virginia.

"Honey?" Virginia motioned with her gun as her heart pounded. She said, "Your dead friend over there called me girlie. See what happened to him? Drop your gun or I plug James, then you. Choose wisely."

The man suddenly cried out. Virginia heard him fall and writhe on the ground. The smell of fecal matter and urine assaulted her nose through the rain and wind. She twisted around and saw the man in a fetal position with uncontrollable bowels screaming in pain. *Terry's handywork with the Shit Releasing Hormone spray. I thought she had run out of it. Where is she?*

James' eyes widened. "What the hell?"

Virginia chuckled. "Bad sushi."

"You're behind this."

"Of course. Now let go of that radio or you will be joining your friend."

James looked confused. "How'd you do it?"

"I told you. Bad sushi"

"Bad sushi my ass." James dropped the radio and reached under his raincoat, pulled out a large, serrated knife and lunged toward Virginia. Three rapid shots rang out as the bullets slammed into his chest. He staggered forward, dropped the knife, then fell face down in the wet sand.

"What the hell?" Virginia looked at her gun and frowned. "I didn't fire."

Terry came around from behind Virginia holding her 9mm Walther pistol and looked down at James' body. "He chose poorly."

"Thanks for that. He did indeed choose poorly. I'll call the Smithsonian for a clean-up crew so there won't be any messy questions by Detective Moon or the sheriff."

Terry's face brightened. "Good idea. Do that while we get cleaned up and dry, then we can go get the treasure."

"After I make the call and examine the quilt again, and we get dry, want to go get some pancakes first?"

"Pancakes? Two men are dead and two will need medical attention soon."

Virginia raised an eyebrow. "And?"

"Okay, pancakes sound good."

Three hours later Virginia and Terry drove up to the steel bridge that transverses over the water from the mainland to Buckman Island. At guard station on the island end of the bridge, she stopped and rolled down her window. Frank, the armed, uniformed guard, stepped out of the concrete guard building.

Frank bent down and looked into the vehicle. "Hello, Ms. Clark, you too, Doctor. The rain finally stopped. There has been quite a lot of activity on Buckman Island since you two went to Galveston. Some of the trucks and the men are still here. I'm glad you told me they were coming. What's going on?"

"They are from the Smithsonian," Virginia said. "They are assisting with some clean-up from our case. They'll be gone before you know it."

Frank straightened and looked at the island. "They said something about bringing a boat back. One of them got away in the storm?"

"Yes. I had them try to find it as well."

"Is Mr. Thornwood involved?"

"Not anymore. He passed away suddenly," Terry said.

"He did? Heart attack?"

"Yes. It stopped abruptly."

"I thought I heard gun shots a while ago. I reported it to the police. They said they knew about it. The officer said a detective told them there was gun fire because of something or another and not to worry about it. I wrote it all in my log."

"Good to know."

"Well, there sure has been a lot of excitement since you two arrived. Henry the Dragon was found, a drug operation was busted, and there was something about fake antiquities. The staff gossips. They think you and Dr. Terry were involved."

Virginia chuckled. "I bet they do. We won't be long, Frank, and then things will settle down."

"Okay, Ms. Virginia. Have a nice rest of your day." As Virginia started to pull away Frank called to her. "Ms. Virginia!"

She backed the car to the guard shack. "What is it, Frank?"

"There is a U.S. marshal at the manor waiting for you." He glanced toward the house. "He said he was looking for you. I hope everything is okay."

"It will be fine. We are expecting him. Thanks for telling us." Virginia accelerated toward the manor.

Virginia and Terry entered the house and found the marshal sitting in the parlor. Virginia stepped forward. "Good afternoon, Marshal. Do you have the warrant?"

"Yes, ma'am." He stood. "I'm Deputy U.S. Marshal Robertson." He handed Virginia the warrant. "The federal judge who issued this said for me to accompany you and Dr. Sorenson to the bank. He said it may make it easier to serve if a federal marshal is with you. Not everyone knows about the Smithsonian Central Security Service."

"That's a good idea," Virginia said. "Can we go now?"

"Yes, Ma'am. There is another deputy marshal at the bank to make sure they don't close before we get there."

"Then let's move. We can follow you."

"My orders are to bring you and Dr. Sorenson. I have emergency signals, and we'll get there faster."

"Lead on, Marshal."

They drove off the island in the marshal's car with the emergency lights and siren on. As they arrived at the bank, Virginia got a text message. She read it and smiled. "We're to meet up at the bank with a Scotland Yard chief inspector. My call to them got through, despite all the red tape."

They pulled up in front of the bank and entered. The bank manager and two other bank personnel met them at the door. A man stood behind them wearing a blue jacket that read U.S. Marshal on it. Next to him, a man in a suit sat in a chair. He stood and walked to Virginia. "I am Chief Inspector McMurry of Scotland Yard. I was instructed to be here when you recover the treasure of King Henry II."

Virginia examined his credentials, then turned to the bank manager. "I know this all seems pretty strange. We have a warrant to open and seize the contents of safety deposit box 1036." She handed the manager the warrant. "You may have a bank lawyer present if you wish."

"He's standing over there by that marshal. We do not see any problem with complying with the court order, Agent Clark." He motioned toward the large safe. "If you step this way, we will get this over with as quickly as possible."

Virginia, Terry, McMurry, and Marshal Robertson followed the manager into the safe. After the bank people unlocked the huge box in the lowest part of the safe, the marshal tugged it out.

"There is another one," said the manager. "It's box 1049."

Virginia sighed. "We'll need another warrant."

"That won't be necessary. When box 1036 was rented, box 1049 was rented as well, and the two boxes were linked together. So, whatever happened to box 1036, the same was good for box 1049. You can open it, too."

Virginia stood shocked. "Are you certain? Has your lawyer been advised?"

"My dear Agent Clark, it was our lawyer who pointed this out and approved it."

"Okay." Virginia motioned this to the marshal, and he and the bank manager opened the new box and pulled it out.

The manager smiled. "I'll wait outside of the vault with the others while you examine the contents." He turned and exited the safe.

Virginia and Terry squatted and opened the covers on the two heavy boxes. They stood and stared at the contents for a minute, then Virginia called to McMurry. "Chief Inspector, here is the long-lost treasure of King Henry II."

Inspector McMurry stepped to the boxes and peered inside. "Yes, I think you have done it. You and Doctor Sorenson have done the Crown a huge favor, Agent Clark. I will notify London and have them assign someone to inventory and verify this." He made a phone call, then returned. "More damn red tape. They will inform me post haste as to the wishes of the Crown."

They looked at the gold and antiquities contained in the boxes when Inspector McMurry's cell phone rang. He looked surprised. "That was fast." He answered his cell phone. "McMurry. What is it, Detective Carpenter?" He listened, then smiled. "Thank you. I will inform Doctor Sorenson and the others." McMurry took a deep breath and slowly let it out. "That was from our Scotland Yard man at the palace. Doctor Sorenson has been requested by the King to oversee the inventorying of the treasure and the verification of it. Someone from the British Museum will be dispatched to assist." He turned to Terry. "Doctor Sorenson, will you accept the request of His Majesty, King Charles III?"

"It would be an honor, Sir. I'll have to ask my boss first."

"Do it, girl! You don't get an opportunity like this every day," Virginia said. "I'll clear it with our director. Dr. Doverspike is going to love this."

McMurry looked concerned. "Are you sure your director will approve?"

Terry chuckled. "Virginia is my boss, and she said yes. And she has Dr. Doverspike wrapped around her little finger. He'll definitely approve if she wants him to." Terry eyed the boxes. "Can I have the treasure moved to my museum in Georgetown, Texas? I have a lab there and equipment to better do the job. And we have tight security."

McMurry thought. "On three conditions. One, I accompany it to your museum. Two, you allow an officer from the Yard to be there to help guard the treasure, and three, and you take me out for your famous Texas barbeque."

"You have a deal," Terry said. "Virginia and I will make the arrangements. This shouldn't take very long."

McMurry sighed. "Texas barbeque. Can't wait. I think I'll buy a cowboy hat while I'm here, too."

Eight weeks later, Virginia and Terry watched the armored car carrying King Henry II's treasure leave the shipping dock at the Georgetown Museum, followed by vehicles containing federal marshals and Scotland Yard officers. Virginia waved at Chief Inspector McMurry, wearing his new cowboy hat, then turned and walked inside with Terry. "So, Doctor, you've been given an award by the King for your work."

"Yes, I'm now a Royal Archaeologist with the title Lady Doctor Sorenson. Has a nice ring. Maybe I'll be able to get a seat at a fancy restaurant easier now. What did His Majesty give you for your work on this case?"

"I am the Lady Partan. I'm now a landed Lord by royal decree of King Charles III. I'm not a peer so I don't get to sit in the House of Lords, but the title is nice. My dear husband, Andy, was impressed, as was my cat."

"What's next on your agenda?"

"Dr. Doverspike mentioned something about me needing to take some vacation before I lose it. So, I'm headed to a quilt retreat on the scenic shores of Lake Ontario in upstate New York. The retreat center is located on the site of an old mansion owned by a prohibition gangster."

ABOUT THE AUTHOR

Dr. David Ciambrone is a retired aerospace and defense company executive, scientist, professor of engineering, and a business and environmental consultant and is now a best-selling, award-winning author, living in Georgetown, Texas. He has published twenty-five (25) books: four (4) non-fiction, two (2) textbooks for a California university, and nineteen (19) mysteries and has two (2) new mysteries in work. He is the author of the Virginia Davies Quilt Mysteries.

Dave has been a speaker at writer's groups, schools, colleges, libraries, quilt guilds, writer's conferences, and business/scientific conferences internationally.

Dr. Ciambrone also wrote three newspaper columns and wrote a column for a business journal.

Dave is a member of Sisters in Crime, the San Gabriel Writer's League, the Writer's League of Texas, Mystery Writers of America, the International Thriller Writers Association, The Beacon Society, and DFW Sherlock Homes Society.

Dave was appointed a U.S. Treasury Commissioner and to the management board of the Resolution Trust Corporation (RTC) by President Clinton.

He is a Fellow of the International Oceanographic Foundation.

Visit David at

Author's Website: davidciambrone.com

Facebook:facebook.com/david.ciambrone?fref=ts

Twitter:twitter.com/mysterywriter5

LinkedIn:linkedin.com/pub/david-ciambrone-sc-d-fiof/11/ab5/bb3

Amazon:amazon.com/author/davidciambrone

Progressive Rising Phoenix Press is an independent publisher. We offer wholesale pricing and multiple binding options with no minimum purchases for schools, libraries, book clubs, and retail vendors. We offer substantial discounts on bulk orders and discounts on individual sales through our online store. Please visit our website at:
www.ProgressiveRisingPhoenix.com

If you enjoyed reading this book, please review it on Amazon, B & N, or Goodreads.
Thank you in advance!

Ingram Content Group UK Ltd.
Milton Keynes UK
UKHW010157010723
424377UK00001B/159